BROOD X

A Firsthand Account of the Great Cicada Invasion

MICHAEL PHILLIP CASH

Disclaimer

The characters and events portrayed in this book are fictitious. Any resemblance to real persons, living or dead is coincidental and not intended by the author.

Red Feather Publishing

New York – Los Angeles – Las Vegas All rights reserved.

ISBN-10: 1-947118-78-1

ISBN-13: 978-1-947118-78-2

Follow Brood X

@michaelpcash

#Brood_X

www.michaelphillipcash.com

www.broodten.com

If you find this book enjoyable, I really hope you'll leave a review on Amazon under Brood X. If you have any questions or comments, please contact me directly at michaelphillipcash@gmail.com.

GRATEFUL ACKNOWLEDGEMENTS

*A special thanks to Mom, Dad, Sharon,
Jennifer, Alexander, Hallie and Cayla.
You're my strength in numbers.*

DEDICATION

*To my brother Eric. When we long for life without
difficulties, you remind me that oaks grow strong in
contrary winds, and diamonds are made under pressure.*

PROLOGUE
FOUND

"What quarrel, what harshness, what unbelief in each other can subsist in the presence of a great calamity, when all the artificial vesture of our life is gone, and we are all one with each other in primitive mortal needs."

- George Eliot

IT WAS BRUTALLY hot in the hospital security room, hotter than Chet could remember. His uniform stuck to his armpits, and he wondered briefly if he smelled. Not that it really mattered, he thought. Who could worry about something like that at a time like this?

Tall, with light green eyes highlighted in a café- au-lait face, he was reality-show handsome. He took out his pick and ran it through his sweat- drenched curls, earning a dirty look from his partner, Ralph.

Overweight with his uniform pulling against his large belly, Ralph McGee was every wife's nightmare of what happens when you drink too much beer.

"Really, Chet?" he remarked sarcastically, looking up from his gray computer screen. "You're worried how your hair looks? Sheesh." He went back to studying the droning monitor and counted five more beds in the corridors of the hospital.

"Looks like zombies attacked Long Island. It's a war zone out there. I hear more are coming in." Chet said grimly. The muffled wail of multiple ambulances could be heard in the distance. "I don't believe this."

"There is no such thing as zombies," remarked Ralph with a smirk.

At least that was true. Zombies only existed in cheesy films and bad books. But these weren't zombies. These were real. It was nature versus us, or really freaks of nature versus humanity.

"I can't see the outside camera," continued Ralph. The radio crackled, but the message was garbled and incomprehensible. His nail-bitten fingers pressed the communication button. "Try again," he said to the speaker. "I can't understand you."

He spun in his seat and pointed to a blank monitor. "Go outside, Chet, and clean off the camera."

"Are you nuts?" Chet shook his head. "That's what we pay you the big bucks for."

Ralph pointed to the door.

There was no way Chet was going outside. Instead he

rolled on his squeaky chair over to the door and opened it to survey the chaos.

The sounds of screams filled the small security room. An overpowering smell of rot caused Chet to gag and slam the door.

"No way, man. I'm not going out there." He rolled back to Ralph, who calmly handed him an open can of soda. Chet took a long swig, sweat beading on his face. "I ain't seen nothing like that in my life."

"Reminds me of sandland in the nineties." "Don't start that, Ralphie. This ain't Iraq and we ain't in the army. Did you see what's going on out there? This is America. It's not supposed to happen here. Man, I wish I could reach my mother. I hope she's OK."

"If she's staying in, she's OK." replied Ralph. "You don't know that. Where were all these people?" Chet pointed to the computer screens with wide eyes. "At a picnic?"

The doorknob jiggled then turned, and both men swiveled to face the portal, fear written all over their faces. No one ever came into security. Not ever.

Chet and Ralph liked to call themselves the invisible men. Nobody sought them out in this sleepy hospital located in a town of a few thousand.

They worked their shift, knowing everybody's business. Every routine from doctors to maintenance people were on their radar, but none of the hospital staff really knew the security guys.

Ralph held his breath. Being the only man armed he put his hand on his side holster. It had been years since he had been in the army, and he didn't practice at the range as much as he would have liked. One time a thug menaced a nurse, and he used his loaded gun to threaten back. That was about it in the last fifteen years.

Jonathan Tate, the EMT from the ambulance unit, entered security and quickly closed the door behind him. Small with narrow shoulders, he looked like an underfed cat. Not a spare ounce of fat covered his body, and his thick blond hair was stuffed into an EMT cap.

He cradled a football-sized object wrapped in bloody linen in one arm. The security guards breathed a sigh of relief.

"You scared the crap outta me," said Ralph as he turned back to his monitor.

"What's that?" Chet pointed at Jonathan's arm. "It's crazy out there!" Jonathan ignored his question. "You got anything to drink?" Chet handed him the unfinished soda. "This is the best you can do?" asked Jonathan.

"Take it or leave it. We ran out of scotch at the last happy hour," interjected Ralph.

They watched him gulp the whole can without coming up for air, fascinated with his gullet riding up and down his neck. His uniform was stained with all kinds of dark matter and blood. Removing the blue cap from his matted hair, he wiped his weary face. "We're dying out there. They just ran out of antibiotics. There's no sign of any arriving for at least a week."

The lights blinked and then went off, along with every-thing else in the room. Green emergency lights bathed their faces for a nanosecond. They collectively froze until the groan of machinery geared up.

"Generators are working," Ralph remarked.

"That's a relief," said Jonathan sarcastically. "Nothing else is. TV is out. Satellite stopped hours ago. You can't get a line out if you tried. It's Armageddon."

"I'd like to see how the insurance companies are going to cover this. You think they have a policy called insect damage?" said Chet.

"Maybe in the Midwest where the crops are," replied Jonathan. "Remember what they did to everyone after the super-storm? Insurance is a joke!"

"You got some more coming in," Ralph interrupted, pointing to the blank screen labeled "exterior." "We heard the sirens." He kicked a rolling chair for the young man to sit down.

"They've moved emergency to the lower garage level," said Jonathan. "Only way down is through the stairwells. They sectioned off the outside completely. Ambulances can get in. That's it. Tents are being set up. It's a mess."

"You smell like, I don't know what you smell like…" Chet wrinkled his nose as Jonathan sat down.

Jonathan looked down at his stained clothing. "I smell like shit and a whole lot more. They're everywhere. I mean,. I think they came from Mars."

"There is no such thing as Martians," said Ralph. He was right again. These weren't zombies, Martians, or the yeti. These were the cicadas. An insect. An invasion that was affecting every state in the northeastern portion of the

United States. A little bug was wreaking havoc on the most densely populated area of America.

"What's your visibility?" asked Jonathan, keeping track of the monitors.

"Zero." Ralph tuned back to the computer screen.

"And for this evening's festivities…" Jonathan pulled off the stained towel and revealed a digital camcorder. Chet and Ralph stared back dumbstruck. The camera could have come from anywhere. "Needs a USB."

"Where'd you get that?" said Chet. "I swiped it out of a patrol car on the expressway."

"Are you stupid? Get rid of it." Chet rolled back from the camera. "Someone could have seen you."

"Right," Ralph said, snatching the camera. He started examining it. "Sissy," he sneered at Chet. "Did you watch it yet?"

"Yeah, in between my manicure and massage," said Jonathan. "I'm stuck here as long as this hospital is up and running. Could be interesting."

"You can't watch that. You got to give it back to the police," Chet interrupted.

"Listen Chet," Jonathan said sternly, "you have anything better to do? We're stuck. They called all EMTs off the road. We can't go anywhere until the army, the government, and the CDC start doing something about those things!"

The room fell deathly silent. Both security guards knew they couldn't leave. There was no going home, probably for a long time. There was no swimming. No baseball. No barbecues. The routine of life as they knew it was gone, and for how long, they could only guess.

"The bugs are stopping all the signals. This might be the only news we're going to get," shouted Jonathan. "It's our duty to watch this."

He felt trapped. For someone in the EMT field, being on the road all day was his office. Jonathan was used to helping people and he loved his new career. Born and raised in Los Angeles, he wondered if there could be a cicada problem there too. He never even remembered noticing these bugs during the summer months.

He moved to Long Island to be with his girlfriend Robin who ran a yoga studio on the south shore. They met on a retreat in Costa Rica, and he left everything to follow her and get a license in the emergency medical field.

There was nothing left he could do for her now. They all had to wait this thing out.

"Or we sit here…safe, for the time being and watch this stupid home video, hoping to see someone make sense outta this thing," said Jonathan.

"It feels wrong," Chet muttered.

"Maybe we'll catch some hot housewife screwing the gardener," said Ralph.

"That's what I'm talking about!" Jonathan laughed.

Ralph and Chet both looked at Jonathan, then at each other. They knew he was right. The truth was they were really stuck.

"Don't you think you should be helping in the emergency room?" Chet pointed to the door.

"According to the Department of Labor, I'm on my break," Jonathan remarked. "You know what happens when we miss our breaks. You want Human Resources in here? Like I said, you're gonna need a USB."

Ralph rummaged through a drawer and found the wire. He yanked one out like he was holding a snake by the neck. He put the plugs where they belonged.

A frozen image of a beautiful two-story home displayed on the monitor. This piqued their interest even further.

"Press play," Jonathan urged as the three heads moved closer to the screen.

"Wait a minute." Ralph leaned back to a maintenance cabinet and pulled out a bottle of bourbon.

"I thought you said we ran out of scotch," Chet accused him.

"You didn't ask about the bourbon." Opening his drawer, he dug out a pack of cigarettes, offering it to each of them, while Chet poured the liquor into specimen cups.

"These been used?" Jonathan asked, looking at the bottom of the cup.

"Yeah, my last drug test." Ralph poured a nice shot and took a swallow. The bourbon went down smoothly.

"And smoking is illegal on hospital grounds too," Chet offered.

"Not only that, it'll kill you," said Ralph after a long drag. "Press 'play,'" he ordered.

Chet moved the cursor to the big arrow button on screen. He clicked play.

All three watched the story unfold.

CHAPTER 1
EXPECTING

"If pregnancy were a book they would cut out the last two chapters."

- Anonymous

"IT'S A BEAUTIFUL day in my, um de dum, a beautiful day...um. Won't you be...? Would...you be...my neighbor?" The disembodied voice sang the butchered Mr. Roger's theme song as the camera panned a peaceful, affluent community.

It was an old-fashioned hamlet, each house nestled on tightly manicured foliage on expensive half-acre plots. The streets were filled with the reckless driving of ninety-nine-pound, perfectly coiffed mommies in their expensive and oversized SUVs. If the speed limit was thirty-five down a residential path, they were pushing at least fifty. The only blot on the horizon was how to fit soccer, ballet, piano, and yoga class between four p. m. and six p. m., so the skinless and boneless chicken would have time to cook to perfection and the quinoa wouldn't be al dente.

Seth, the singer of this charming ditty, took his new camera on a tour of his property. Small patches of snow covered the lawn, remnants of an unusually early November snowstorm that happened two weeks ago.

Although it was chilly outside after that freak weather event, it had been unseasonably mild. "It was funny," Seth mused. The anchors on television had turned weather into newsworthy items: rain was an event, storms became a "super-event," and snowstorms and the media were on a first-name basis.

He looked at a tree on his property. Magnolia buds had stupidly started sprouting.

As he spoke, his breath floated before the lens of the camera. "Casa de Fletcher, baby."

An attractive home, it was made lovingly with yellow siding, deep red brick, and a rolling front lawn. The sun was hanging low, its weak light peeking through bare branches of the cherry tree.

Seth ambled to the front door, still humming. A silver "number one" dangled off a single nail.

Touching it with a finger, he watched the late after-noon light reflect off its shiny surface.

"Hmm, I thought I fixed that. Oh well," he chuckled. Bouncing the screen door against the jam, he laughed at the groaning springs. "Guess I have to fix that too." Still filming, he tried to get it to align with his knee, in a half-hearted attempt to get it to close properly. "Looks like the bugs are getting in this year. Note to self: stock up on bug spray."

Unlocking the door, he walked into a warmly decorated foyer filled with the junk of newlywed dreams. An antique school clock frozen at eleven o'clock dominated one wall. It had been their first big expense, and they got it in Connecticut on a road trip. Next to it, an old milk jug molded from local clay held dry flowers. It was full of lead and other contaminants. He wondered briefly if the poison in the clay affected kids a hundred years ago.

On an opposite wall hung a couple of their wedding shots in artsy black and white. He didn't get it; color was so much more natural. Then came a few candid vacation shots and of course the obligatory parents' pictures. He and his mom caught in a feral snarl that passed as a smile. The Cleaver family picture, right out of a episode—Lara, her two older brothers, and Ward and June in front of the tree—and no, it couldn't be, all in matching reindeer sweaters. He shuddered thinking about that first Christmas he met the parents and their android sons.

The homey clatter of pots being filled with water drifted from the kitchen. His wife was moving ever so efficiently at the granite counter, totally absorbed in the process of making dinner.

Man, he loved her ass. She was wearing black yoga pants and a tight wifebeater, well, really a husband-beater T-shirt. Her black hair was pulled into a sloppy bun held together with a scrunchie. She either just finished at the yoga studio or got home from school early. Lara taught third grade locally and loved it.

In a sibilant whisper he shared with his silent audience, "And rarely seen, a Long Island housewife is gathering her catch to make dinner."

"Seth! You scared me." She spun around smiling, enjoying his joke.

Seth continued, "Though usually camera-shy, these sophisticated hunters rely on their great skill of calling out for delivery…"

"Veggies and baked chicken cutlets," she said with an effervescent smile.

"Me want sushi." Seth hit his chest with his free hand and grunted like an ape.

"I cooked. We're eating home. Where did you get that?" She pointed her wooden spoon at the camera. Lara's eyes shone with inner excitement.

"Hey, take off your clothes, put on your apron, and I can tape us both cooking." He nuzzled her neck as the camera filmed the lower cabinets.

"Cooking what?" she said with a laugh.

"We could sweat the onions." His voice became a sexy whisper. "Hot and steamy vegetables sound right." He pulled the camera up as his lips moved to the back of her neck. "I know just how I want to roast my meat…"

"And I can butter your buns." She spun around and quickly kissed him back. "No, I think not.

Chicken cutlets, skinless. And dry vegetables for you, my boy. We want to stay healthy." She gave him a tender smile.

"We? When did you become French? Oui, we?" "I'd like to see France one day." Her large blue eyes misted over. Seth looked at his wife, really looked at his wife. She was gorgeous. Snow White in the flesh. Her porcelain skin glowed, jet black hair, ruby red lips, and she was all his.

"Why, why, why? I ask you for the thousandth time. Why do we want to stay healthy?" Seth whined as he backed away. "So we give up red meat, wheat, butter, pasta, and sugar. What's left?"

"Bulgur," said Lara.

"Then instead of dessert, to top it off we run and run and run. For what, I have no friggin' idea. A few extra days? Months, maybe? By the time you give everything up, death looks like a picnic."

"Stop that. How did the interview go?" Lara questioned.

"How d'ya think?" He dropped the camera on the kitchen counter. It was a partial picture, just their torsos.

"Do you think they'll call you back?" Lara asked hopefully.

"Nah. I left. I saw all these old salesmen types. You know, like Willy Loman, the loser from — blech! I even saw some Realtors there too. It was too depressing. They need a job more than me."

" need you to get a job," she implored. "Something will turn up. Someday." Seth started picking at the chopped vegetables. They were tasteless. She was really the worst cook in the world.

Lara sighed gustily and replied, "Someday is not a day of the week." She tried hard not to show her disappointment.

Lara knew he didn't want to work. He never seemed

this lazy when they were dating. But two years into marriage, his passion for his job seemed to recede.

"Why do you have a camera?"

"Sex tape."

"Why do you have a camera?" Lara persisted. "You're jobless, and you still went out and bought a camera."

"I tried Mitch's camera. I loved it! Look at this thing. We can be like Kim and Kanye. Kimye! Lara and Seth. Lareth! Or Sera."

Lara didn't know what to say. Water boiled over and broke the uncomfortable silence.

"Can I help you look for a job?" Lara said in a small voice as she turned off the stove.

"You can help me dip shrimp tempura rolls in soy sauce." He looked over at the boiling pot of veggies. "Ruined! The vegetables are ruined!" he shouted dramatically. "Ruined, I say! Save me from a bad meal." He dropped to his knees. "Save me, Lara." Then in a pathetic voice, "Puh-lease."

"You're impossible. I mean, I have to deal with twenty screaming eight-year-olds all day and then one big eight-year-old all night." She brushed his light brown curls from his forehead. She loved his jade green eyes and the scruffy day-old beard he was sporting.

"I don't know what I'm going to do with you. And a stupid camera too!" She shut off the oven, defeated, and turned to go into the direction of the bedroom.

"Wait here, I have something special for you." She smiled slyly.

Seth snatched the camera from the counter. Glancing back, she noticed Seth was now filming her tush. "Stop filming my behind." He moved the camera slowly up her beautiful body.

"Now!" She smiled with as much seriousness as she could muster. Lara quickly left.

"Sushi time!" Seth roared. He smirked to himself, thinking he always got his way. Lara was so easy.

"Turn it on, Seth!" Lara was screaming from the other room.

"What? Turn you on? Lareth, here I come," he called back.

"Turn on the camcorder!" Her voice was louder, almost shrill.

"It is on. I never turned it off."

"Get ready. I have a surprise," Lara crooned.

With images of his wife in the kinky, crotchless maid outfit he bought for Valentine's Day, Seth readied the lens for her entrance. He was thinking of where they could screw. They'd had sex dozens of times on the kitchen table. He wanted today to be different. He wanted to film the entire thing. Seth thought the camera actually turned her on.

Screwing on film for the first time. "Well, well, well, this is gonna be great," he said to himself.

He wondered if the cologne he put on in the morning before the interview would have lasted this long. "Thank goodness I showered today," he thought. Seth was ready for sex. No foreplay. No kissing. Just a hot wife willing to drop to her knees at the sight of Seth holding the camera.

Lara spun into view. No kinky crotchless underwear.

No thigh-highs. Not even her leather miniskirt. She was still in the same yoga pants and white T-shirt. It didn't matter to Seth. He would still have sex with his wife even if she didn't shower for a week. He loved the hell out of her. He would have enjoyed her more right now if she was naked, but he would screw her any which way she wanted for the first time on camera.

"Ta-da!" Lara held up a pink wand looking like Vanna White revealing the answer on .

"Whaaaat?" Seth looked for a clue and came up with nothing. "Is that a vibrator?" he said, hopelessly titillated.

"What?" Lara said, shocked those words could have come from her husband's mouth. "Seth!" she hissed.

"We can use a vibrator for our first porno. I'm cool with that."

"What!?"

"What's up, baby?"

"That's right!" Lara's face shifted from pissed to a euphoric grin. "Baby."

Seth didn't get it. She tried again.

"Baby!" she shouted and waltzed around the room, waving the wand. "No sushi, caffeine, or alcohol…"

"No sushi, caffeine, or…what the fu…"

"I took an EPT test earlier. You know, just because I've been so erratic lately."

"What the fu…"

"Yes, Seth," she smiled, her whole face lighting up as she looked into the camera. "They say babies bring luck."

Seth slowly stood up. She didn't know whether he was

going to cry with tears of happiness or tears of sorrow. Their marriage had been a bit more difficult lately, especially with Seth out of work.

Lara had daydreamed about this moment since the first day she met him.

However, in that scenario Seth was working and making a ton of money. She was unsure of his reaction. They'd dealt with pressure before, especially the wedding. Lara's family wanted to run the whole show from Arizona, complete with circus clowns and a rodeo. Both he and Lara had wanted something more low-key, but she couldn't say no to her parents. They had strange parental guilt tactics and usually ended up controlling any and all situations.

Trying to be as cute as possible, Lara wiggled her butt around the room to lighten the impact for Seth. His reaction could have gone either way.

He approached her. Lara had a quick vision in her head of Seth as a new father. She pursed her lips and thought, "Maybe, just maybe, this will make him grow up."

Seth wrapped his arms around Lara and faced the camera so they were both in the picture. "If I had any more luck, Lara, I'd be a leprechaun."

She looked into his eyes and asked earnestly, "Are you happy?"

He kissed her forehead, her cheeks, and the tip of her nose. "I am the happiest man alive."

That was why Lara really loved him so much. He understood her, really cared. Nestling in his embrace, she felt warm and protected. He had a cavemanish thing going.

Lara adored him. She would adore his baby. A job would come when it came. Right now, she was the happiest she had felt in a while.

Looking into the lens of the camera, Seth stated, "It was fate that I bought this camera today, son."

Lara looked up at him with a furrowed brow.

"Son?" Lara asked. "Who are you talking to?" "I am making a documentary for our son."

He pointed the lens at Lara's very flat stomach. "Your first picture, my boy, and you didn't even have to wait in line at Sears. So let's see. It's November now, Alvin."

"Wait, what?" said Lara as she backed slowly away. "Alvin? I don't think so, and what makes you so sure it's a boy?"

"That's what I do, ma'am." Seth hitched up his pants and drawled like a cowboy. "I make boys.

Back to my documentary. Your mom doesn't like Alvin… how about Brutus?"

"Brutus?" Lara remarked. "Seth, we live in Oyster Bay not Rome during Caesar's rule."

"Well, I have a whole alphabet to test out. As I was saying November, December, January…" He counted the remainder of the months with his free hand. "I'd say, Clem, you're going to be a summer baby. Yep. By my expert calculations, I think we can expect an August arrival."

"Seth, stop." Lara pushed the camcorder away from her midsection. "We're not naming our kid Clem. That's crazy. And radiation is not good for the baby."

"This thing doesn't emit radiation." "Seth." Lara tried to get serious with him.

Stroking his arms, feeling maternal, she looked into his eyes and said softly, "If I have to lug him around for nine months, his name is my choice. Names are important. They define a person. We have to really think about it," she said solemnly. "I want a perfect pregnancy."

"Everything about you is perfect. Let's go get supplies."

Finally an action plan she approved. Supplies were good, and besides, they could use some junk food in the house.

"I need ice cream and potato chips," said Lara. "What about your frozen veggie mix?"

* * *

Dressed warmly, they exited the front door into the early evening. Seth was still filming her delicious ass in her yoga pants. The Ugg boots added an even sexier appeal, not to mention the North Face jacket and slouchy wool hat. Seth knew she was perfect for him. The fact that now he pictured her holding his baby, that there were three people leaving the house, made Seth all the happier. "Yes," he thought, "I feel happy." It was a novel idea. He hadn't felt content for a long time.

The midsize Mercedes SUV was generally parked in the garage, but Seth had wanted to test out his new toy around the front of the house. He liked making a grand entrance.

As they entered the car, Seth handed the camera off to Lara. She obliged and took it from him.

"It can't just be the Lara show. Dexter will want to see his father when he watches this."

"You are not picking the names anymore." "Dexter is a classic name. He sounds like aprofessional poker player already. I could see him winning the world series."

"Dexter is a murderer!" Lara looked him straight in the eye and questioned, "Dexter Fletcher?" They both shook their heads and said "nah" together.

They headed down their quaint street and turned left onto the main drag of Oyster Bay. Small mom-and-pop shops filled the homey shopping center. Streetlights started popping on, giving the community an embracing quality. There were no franchises. Most stores were boutiques opened by bored women whose husbands worked like dogs.

There was the ubiquitous Starbucks, which was packed with after work latte drinkers.

A music school, art school, "Lil' Chef" school— Seth had never noticed so many storefronts dedicated to children. Who paid for all that stuff? Where were they going to get it from? Maybe they'd have to give up the Benz for a cheaper car. Minivan, anyone? Seth's warm and fuzzy feeling from a minute ago started to evaporate.

He considered what his mother provided for him: a bed, food, and a slap when he whined. No, no, his son was going to be brought up around the finer things in life. More than that, he resolved tofind patience. His son would be brought up in a much nicer home than the one where he came from. He looked across at Lara, his eyes softening. She would see to that. He caressed her knee and she giggled, her eyes playful. Yup, this was going to be great.

"Whaddya say, burger first?" Seth said as he wiggled his eyebrows at her. "We need red meat. Let's go to the diner."

"S'mores… I could really go for s'mores. In fact," she continued, "I think I'm craving them."

"I can tell you one thing, Lara Chaney Fletcher, my boys can swim."

"Watch the road, Mr. Dad."

"Dad. I like it. Wait." Seth picked up his cell phone. "I gotta let Neil know."

Lara didn't want to hear the name Neil. The evening was going perfectly. Seth's reaction was great. But every time he spoke to Neil, he just got stupid. Really stupid.

This was the same Neil who taught Lara's husband how to do a keg stand the first night she met Seth in college.

"Neil. Neil? Really? Don't you think we should call your mother and my parents first? I know my parents are going to want to fly out for this."

"Just the reason not to call them. I think we should notify them sometime next September. By snail mail. We'll stop at the post office. Get some stamps."

"You are unreal," said Lara. "Telling your friend before we tell family."

Seth gripped the steering wheel with his knee.

He started banging out a text message to his friend. The car swerved, snapping Lara out of her epic pout.

"Please be careful," Lara begged. "I don't want to crash and die with a zygote in my belly because you have the sudden urge to call the kid who slept with all your ex-girlfriends."

"And you should be happy he did, my dear," Seth replied. "If he didn't, maybe I would have ended up with one of them, living a horribly miserable existence. Instead I have my sweet honey and my son, Dawson, sitting with me." "We did the letter D already." "Sorry, Ebenezer."

Lara snorted. She could never tell when Seth was joking or when he was serious. There was no possible way he was naming his kid Ebenezer.

Right?

The cell phone rang in the car, and Neil's name popped up on Seth's cell screen as he showed it off to Lara.

"Our first call!" Seth said, trying to get his wife more involved. "Do you want to let him know?"

"I would rather tell a stranger."

Lara got a knot in her stomach. She knew it wasn't because of the pregnancy. She hated when Seth was trying to reenact his college days.

She sank into her typical hushed anger. Ignoring her, he touched "accept" and put the phone up to his ear.

"For Chrissake, use your Bluetooth," said Lara.

"You're gonna get a ticket."

"Dude!" the voice boomed through the other side of the phone. Neil was so loud that Lara could hear every word sitting in the passenger seat.

"I know!" roared Seth. "Dude. Dude! Really, dude. Seems like only yesterday we were in Hell Week. Now check me out!"

Hell Week was the final week of pledging at Long Island University. Seth and Neil had formed a special bond.

They were both womanizers and loved to flirt with all the freshman girls. Sleeping with one of these guys was a rite of passage for any newbie in college.

But Lara saw something different in Seth. She trusted him and felt protected by him.

Seth was beaming. Lara was steaming.

A police siren blared in the background. Lara turned to see the flashing red and blue lights.

"Seth, you're being pulled over!" exclaimed a nervous Lara. "Hang up the phone!" she urged.

Seth glanced through the rearview mirror. "Shit," he said. "I gotta jump. Sorry, man. Cop nailed me. Later."

Lara was relieved the conversation didn't last more than thirty seconds, hating it when they spoke. She had him now, and she wasn't sharing him with some loser who wasn't even thinking about growing up, moving on, or getting married. Neil was not a good influence.

Seth looked at Lara. He had seen her face like that before. He wasn't going to give the furrowed brow behind the camera a chance to discipline him.

"Don't even think of saying it," said Seth with innocent eyes. "Ebenezer shouldn't hear you demean his father."

He repeated the name Ebenezer with different inflections. Lara thought he was really considering such a weird name. Seth liked keeping Lara on her toes; it was a very primal relationship. He just loved to mess with her. She was so gullible, he thought with a grin.

"Don't worry," he confided. "I got this."

The police officer leaned down and knocked his

knuckle on the window. Seth pressed the button, and the window glided down. Clean-shaven with aviator glasses covering his eyes, the officer had a cushy job giving young upwardly mobile brats tickets in this community.

"Papers," the officer demanded tonelessly. "Scissors," came the pithy reply.

Seth motioned cutting paper with two fingers. "Scissors beats paper. Paper loses. Scissors wins, yay." He smiled sweetly up at the officer and looked at his nametag. "Officer Simon."

Lara poked Seth, but he was immune to common sense.

The officer was not amused either. "It is illegal to talk on your cell phone while driving," said the officer. "Papers, sir."

"Officer Simon, I was relaying some exciting news to my buddy." Seth lifted Lara's left arm like a champion. "My missus just announced she's pregnant."

Officer Simon narrowed his eyes. "License and registration. Now," was the terse reply.

Seth dropped Lara's arm. Apparently the officer wasn't as delighted as Seth expected. Leaning over, he shuffled through the papers in the glove compartment. "I don't know why they call it a glove compartment," he grumbled. "I don't use gloves."

"Calm down," Lara urged.

Seth responded in a stage whisper. "I am calm. He is ruining the moment. I hope you're filming this for Fredrich."

Lara was miserable that a cop had stopped their car, but she had to admit she was more relieved that Seth appeared to be over the name Ebenezer. She thought for a second about Fredrich but only hoped he was still joking.

Seth snapped out the vehicle papers to the officer. Visibly annoyed, he unbuckled his seat belt and dove deep into his pocket. He yanked his wallet from his jeans, slipped out his beat-up driver's license, and handed it to the cop. "I couldn't help it, I was excited."

"You can be excited," said the cop. "You can't break the law."

"Guess we all have to do what…" He looked at the officer's nametag. "Simon says."

"You're too dependent on your cell phone. Try powering down for a while. It'll be a revelation."

"Yeah, yeah," Seth said, not trying too hard to piss off the cop. "Gimme the ticket."

The officer walked back to his car.

"You are being so rude," Lara whispered angrily. "You have to relax. Besides," she said with giddiness, "what will Hector think?" She patted her belly.

A slow smile tugged at Seth's mouth. She always knew how to jolly him out of his sullen mood. She was a good wife in that she never compounded his misery. If something was bothering him, Lara would never dare put salt on the wound—unless, of course, it was about her family. She would do anything for her side. He had to admit she was fair; she always protected his mom as well. Someone had to. After all, his mom was alone, and Lara felt bad for her because she was a perfect daughter and chose to be a perfect daughter-in-law too.

Seth snapped back to his foul mood and looked back at the cop. "What's the hold up with this guy?"

The officer returned and handed Seth the ticket.

"Eight hundred dollars!" Seth was outraged. "You should be ashamed."

The cop saluted Seth and made his way back to his squad car. Seth wasn't done mocking though. He always wanted to get the last word in, even if he knew he was wrong.

"Well, there goes our boy's college education," Seth said a little louder than he should have. "Looks like apprenticeship, son. Think he'll be a good shoemaker or a mechanic?"

Lara giggled. Seth handed her the ticket, and she put it in her purse.

Seth said in a condescending tone, "Give up your cell phone. The nerve of these people."

He started the car in a huff and continued their drive.

CHAPTER 2

HEED

"Everything is funny as long as it is happening to somebody else."

- Will Rogers

"I SAID ACTION." Lara and Seth were in their small but cozy den. A seventy-inch flat screen lit up the room. Lara was draped across her end of the light green couch. It was tough to distinguish where her skin started and where the couch ended.

"Yuck," Lara moaned, "I'm still nauseous. The crackers did nothing." Resting on a huge pillow, she buried her head in her arms.

"Come on, Lar. You look beautiful. I want to show off our two-month baby bump. Zebidiah will want to see it."

"You skipped X," Lara said as a matter of fact.

"No I didn't. I called him Xenia at breakfast." "Xenia's a girl's name."

"No girl's names allowed," said Seth. "So then we'll call him Xenio."

"That's a made-up name," Lara said, lifting her head up. She was a little more congested now.

Never having suffered with allergies, the pregnancy created hormonal surges that had the weirdest results. Her nose was stuffed up. "We said no

made-up names."

"You said Hercules!" Seth accused. "Hercules isn't a made-up name."

"It was a movie character played by Ah-nold. That would be like me saying Frodo."

"Hercules was still a real person. Frodo was a Hobbit… why are we fighting about this?"

She scratched an itch on her side and slowly pulled herself off the couch. Straightening up, she lifted a gray sweatshirt revealing a perfect baby bump.

"You look like Angelina Jolie. Only shorter. And with smaller lips. And no tattoos…"

"And no Brad Pitt," Lara interrupted. "I don't think the whole pregnancy thing is fair. The universe must really hate women for doing this to us. You get distinguished as you get older. We get dowdy. We get periods, leg and chin hair. What do you get?"

"We get to be heroes to our pregnant wives."

"I have to push a watermelon out of my vagina, Seth." Lara sniffed. "If that's not superhuman, I don't know what is."

"Yeah, but we…"

A special news report flashed on the television in red, and for a moment their argument stopped.

"Shush. Did something happen?" Lara interrupted him.

"I have no idea," replied Seth. "Don't you think Iron Man could deliver a baby too?"

"Seth, I want to watch this." She turned her attention to the television.

"Welcome back to our special report, 'Infestation—The New Reality. '" The news anchor sat in the studio, her face grim.

"Isn't on?" said Seth.

"Stop," said Lara. "She looks pretty serious." "Infestation? Are they talking about those stupid bed bugs again?"

An image of a beautiful garden was displayed on TV. The anchor continued, "In just a few months, the trees will be turning a leafy green. The flowers, ready to bloom. It looks like those beady-eyed bugs are arriving in time for summer. These bugs are not going to bring the gentle summer sounds this year. Here's Ted Logan with our top story."

Lara batted Seth and his camera away while documentary footage played of cicadas on trees.

"Their noise can be deafening," the voice said over the footage. "Their erratic flight paths and their presence, simply unwelcome."

The reporter walked up the steps of a convenience store in a small town on Long Island.

Holding up a mike to an older man wearing a VFW cap, he started asking questions. The man looked annoyed.

"Yeah, I'm ready for them," he stated firmly. "They come every year."

"While they do come every year, this year is going to be quite different. They are gross, they crawl and fly. Like it or not, Brood Ten is coming, by the billions, and staying around all summer long. As the weather warms up, so does their activity."

Ted turned to interview a young girl with braces.

She was camera shy and awkward. "Are you scared?" Clusters of people surrounded the mike.

"I don't like the noise they make," the girl said with a distressed voice.

"That's their distinctive mating call. Because we're expecting so many of them, it's going to be louder than ever before," the reporter said.

"That's really scary," the girl replied.

Ted, a textbook and gruff news reporter, scanned the outskirts of a wooded area with microphone in hand

"Brood Ten is like no other infestation. It is a species of cicadas with the greatest range and concentration of any other insect. Its invasion zone is expected to stretch north of Boston to south of DC. After being asleep for nearly two decades, emergence from the deep soil is inevitable."

An extreme close-up of a cicada was displayed on TV. It took over the whole screen with its large, protruding red eyes and thick black body. The well- veined wings fluttered, its shivering body making a familiar rattle and hum.

"Eew. They're creepy," said Lara.

"So you really like the names Jacob or Edward?" said Seth, still in his own world.

"Gross." Lara's eyes were glued to the program. "I know. I hated too."

"I'm not talking about ." She pointed emphatically to the television. "I'm talking about those hideous things on TV."

"Haven't you seen a cicada before?" Seth said calmly. "They are always here in the summer."

"No," Lara noted abruptly. "Well, I never noticed them before."

The interview began with a local somewhere in upstate New York. Ted held the microphone up.

"Have you ever heard of a cicada?" asked Ted. "Of course," the man replied. "They come out at the beginning of summer."

Lara looked at Seth through the corner of her eye. He smirked knowingly at Lara. "See."

"Cicadas are those bugs that make a rattlesnake sound toward the end of the season."

"Locusts?" the man questioned.

"No, sir, cicadas are not locusts. People often confuse both insects. Are you preparing for an emergence of Brood Ten this summer? Our prediction is for billions of cicadas to emerge from under the ground."

This threw the man for a loop. He started showing signs of restlessness. "Well, now you've gone and mentioned about the cicada, how do you prepare for something like that?" He ended this question with a laugh that ended up as a wheeze.

The screen cut to a professor's office. Benjamin Hawkner, a noted entomologist, filled the screen. He was gangly with a shock of bright red hair, his face filled with freckles. He looked more like Carrot Top than a world-renowned scientist. Wearing a white lab coat, he nervously played with his pair of horn-rimmed glasses. Behind him was a large poster of a cicada with all its vitals identified. Every organ had a tiny definition next to it. He had rows of display cases with thousands of insects pinned to boards.

Dr. Hawkner spoke directly into the camera. "Despite our advanced civilization and technology, cicadas represent a reminder that there are certain things in nature beyond our control. Unfortunately we cannot do anything to stop this emergence and coming invasion. I expect ten to twenty million per square mile throughout the entire Northeast."

"This is creeping me out." Lara nodded to the scientist.

"He's creeping me out," Seth said.

"Are they dangerous?" Ted questioned, taking the words right out of Lara's mouth.

"Cicadas do not generally bite but may mistake a person's skin for a tree. Cicadas have a long proboscis or snout under their head, which they implant into bark and plant stems in order to feed on sap. It can be quite excruciating if they attempt to pierce a person's skin with it."

"Female cicadas on the other hand will attempt to lay their eggs everywhere, even a person's skin. This could cause agonizing pain. Using a stinger," he said and pointed to the enlarged illustration of the insect's stinger, "called the ovipositor, the females of the species make an incision and insert roughly five hundred eggs into the slit."

"Yikes!" Seth shuddered. "That's gotta hurt."

Ted asked the scientist, "Cicadas come every year, why is this Brood different?"

Dr. Hawkner paused for a minute then sighed and explained, "This Brood is different because they have been dormant for nearly two decades. Building strength and resistance to predators, they will be tunneling en masse and I'm fearful we will not be able to handle the multitudes."

As the scientist continued to prep the viewers, Seth leaned in and pressed his thumb on Lara's neck, buzzing loudly.

Lara shrieked and ran away screaming. Seth was now lying on the couch, rolling with laughter. She was such an easy mark.

Lara stood in the doorway. "You suck! That was so mean, Seth." She was clearly pissed with her husband.

Seth just laughed harder. "Oh, come on, Lar! Can't you take a joke? It's a bug, a tiny insect. We crush bugs!"

"Are you deaf or just stupid?" Lara asked. "Apparently there is a cicada disaster on the horizon, but you could give two shits."

"No, Lara. I don't give one shit."

"Oh, big man, Seth. What about the baby?" she whined.

Seth's eyes softened behind the camera as he looked at his nervous wife. He knew she was a nut when it came to safety, but this, Seth believed, was just absolutely ridiculous.

"I planted my eggs in you and it made you pretty happy," Seth said in a cocky tone.

"Idiot. It was sperm."

"Sperm, eggs, what's the difference." Then, in an imitation she'd heard one too many times of a foreign dictator, Seth piped, "I veel take zees bugs and crush zem as da vermin zey are!"

This time around, his humor was lost on Lara. "Cut it out Seth."

"Wasn't there a swarm of locusts that recently invaded Egypt? I read that on Google News. C'mon Lara, it ended up being a footnote in world events. Remember those annoying stinkbugs that appeared out of nowhere last year? We paid that guy four hundred dollars to get rid of them."

They could both try and jolly each other out of their misery, but the news made the situation a bit too serious. He could find a job anytime. They could afford to get by, just barely. But that didn't worry Lara. What worried her was the information she had just heard.

How in the world was she going to have a baby with an infestation of this magnitude? Lara folded her arms across her chest clearly out of patience with her juvenile husband. She pivoted and stormed off.

* * *

Seth lay dozing on the couch, Oprah droning on in the background. He was in the beautiful twilight place of not quite sleep, but not quite awake. The most restful place he could be. The blare of a horn startled him and he cursed loudly and thoroughly.

Realizing the sound was coming from his own garage he knew that it only meant trouble. Lara would never do that unless there was a problem. He sprinted for the door without even putting on shoes. It was cold outside. Lara sat frozen in the front seat, her eyes dilated with fear, a giant yellow lab resting his paws on the driver side window.

Panting playfully, long strands of drool ran a giant spider web from his snout to the car.

"Casey," Seth walked down and grabbed the dog by a red bandana collar. "Lara, what's the matter with you. It's only Casey, Jeff and Cathy's dog."

She shook her head. "Casey's a puppy." She wasn't going to come out until the dog was gone.

"I've got him, Lar. It really is Casey. He's a big boy now. Come on out, he won't hurt you."

She slowly opened the door and the dog went wild with excitement. Seeing Lara's unease, Seth restrained the dog. "Down boy. He likes you, Lar. He wants to play."

"Well I don't want to play with him." She protectively covered her belly.

"You didn't mind last summer."

"He was half the size and calmer. Take him across the street. I don't want him to jump on me," she ordered petulantly.

She was crabby today. "Tired?"

"So tired. I don't even want to eat. I'll see you later. I'm going to lie down," Lara yawned.

"You okay, babe?" Seth asked with a hint of alarm.

Lara smiled. "Yep, it's your son that's wearing me out. You take care of dinner, do you mind? I don't care what you make."

"Consider it done. But first I am taking this young man back to his parents."

Seth walked across the street to the neighbor and tapped their door.

Cathy, a forty something, slightly overweight, blond reached out and took the dog by the collar.

"What happened?" she smiled indulgently at her dog.

"He frightened Lara. She didn't realize it was Casey. He got so big."

"He's a monster. I don't know what I'm gonna do with him. He disappeared into Jimmy's yard yesterday and his mom really complained."

"Better get him spayed," Seth offered. She cocked her head at him. "Calms them down. They're not as frisky," he continued.

"Ouch. I don't know if I really want to do that to him. I mean it feels cruel. He's harmless," Cathy responded. "Jeff's in the back, you want some coffee?"

"Thanks, I gotta go." Seth shrugged and patted the dog on his head. "Yeah, but think about the neutering, Cath, it keeps them out of trouble. Say hello to Jeff." He turned and wondered briefly if Lara would enjoy eggs for dinner.

CHAPTER 3
PREP

"Plan to be spontaneous tomorrow."

- Steven Wright

"HI, MOM." SETH answered the phone while he was eating a salami sandwich. "Yup, fine. Nope, nope. Been there. I got months of unemployment left."

Lara walked into the room, mouthing, "Who's that?" as she pointed to the phone. The camera was charging on the counter.

"Lara says hi, Mom."

Lara rolled her eyes. Seth motioned for the receiver, and Lara fervently shook her head no.

"Yeah," he smiled, "she's cute. No, we don't want to know." There was a long pause. "Because. Because we just don't. Look, Ma, you can do things your way; I do things my way. Yup, Lara agreed. Do you want to ask her?"

Lara held out both her hands in terror and shook her head negatively.

Seth still held out the receiver to her. Lara took it with defeat.

She perked up and said cheerily, "Hi, Maureen. Great. We're great. Soon, getting big." She stared daggers at Seth, who picked up the camera and happily filmed her.

"Thanks, but I picked out a crib. Yeah, we bought it. Why? Seth says it's nothing to worry about. Um…like the killer bees in Arizona. They come and they go. Yes, I know, you'll come the first week of September. Yes, my parents will be gone. Of course you can bring Roy. I don't have a problem…"

Seth muttered, "Ugh!" and Lara warned him to be quiet with a finger over her lips.

"Of course you can be Nana. My mom will be fine with that. Yes, yes. Ha, you're funny. OK, bye now. Love ya."

"What was that all about?" asked Seth.

"She's heard about the impending cicada outbreak. She was a little nervous."

"My mom was nervous?"

"Hard to believe but she asked if we want to come out there for a while."

"No, no, a thousand times no!"

Lara smiled. "Eventually we are going to have to visit her." She started going through their mail. "Look, this one's for you."

She handed him a flyer on bug extermination. "It says here they can do something about the infestation."

"Yeah, sure, and so could I for a thousand bucks!"

"I'm just saying," Lara retorted.

"Look at these prices. I'm going back to school to become an exterminator." Seth scanned the price sheet.

Lara kept handing him envelopes.

"Look at all this stuff." He leafed through a ton of mail. "Chimney caps to prevent bug home invasion, repellent. Look at this one, cute cozies to cover the bottom of the door so the bugs can't get in. Ha, Lara, this guy created a cicada jail." In a huckster's voice he read the ad, "Bug out with Bugster's. They've created a cottage industry out of this."

"Seth, let's call one of them to find out what they're offering."

Seth moved to the garbage and dropped all the mail in the trash. "Bug off," he said to her with a smile.

* * *

The examination room was cold. "Come on, Lara. As far as I'm concerned, there's only one way for this to conclude, and that's the birth of our bouncy baby boy, Ronald."

"You mean Sven." The camera swung around to a pregnant Lara in a blue paper gown, legs splayed on the examination table. "Do you have to point the camera there, Seth? I mean, really? Maybe I'm going to have to do some filming myself. 'Mr. Drools when he sleeps.' Oh, by the way, since you have that job interview, Marni would like to take your place at that Lamaze class. I mentioned it to you last week, but you didn't answer me."

"We were speaking about that this week?" "Last week I was. You weren't listening." "I don't recall that."

"Exactly." Lara pleated her paper gown, trying to fold over a tiny tear.

"Oh yeah, right. Marni." Seth suddenly remembered.

"You sure you still want Marni as Godmama for Tyrone?"

"She's my oldest friend."

"Older than dirt," said Seth, a little too harshly. "Do you think her herpes adds to her value as the guardian of Uriah's soul?"

"Stop."

"I mean do you think Father Felix is going to be over-joyed with your choice?" Seth continued to push.

"Don't go there."

"If she touches the baptism water, do you think it'll boil?"

"You are not funny."

"Did you know that the character of Al Pacino in the was based on Marni?"

"She's good…" "In bed."

"How would you know?" Lara asked with tightened lips.

"I've heard."

"From whom?" Lara was getting more serious. "From Lance, Ethan, Nick, Josh, Robert, Max,

Eric, Matthew, Jason, Cooper, Brody, Kevin…" "OK, I get it."

"Paul, Billy, Alexander, David, Carl, Vinnie, Stu, Frank…"

"Oh…kay!"

"Want me to continue? I think I got about a third of

the way through," said Seth. "I believe there's a list some-where in the men's bathroom in Riggs Hall."

"I was saying she's a good soul and a dear friend.

We all should think how we'd appear under scrutiny." This was said with a knowing look that would have shamed most men. But most men were not Seth.

"Speak for yourself, madam. I am as pure as the driven snow." Seth placed his hand over his heart earnestly.

Lara couldn't help the snort that escaped her nostrils, along with the uncontrollable gas that came with preg-nancy. Seth lost it, and Lara couldn't help herself either.

The hysterical laughter caused the camcorder to shake with the advent of more gas.

"Eewww! Quit it!" exclaimed Seth.

"Stop, you're making me fart," Lara said with uncon-trollable giggles, her face bright red. Seth knew how to up the ante even more.

"Any husband would have left you if he heard someone fart like that."

She started taking a breath to calm down.

Seth started riling her up more. "I would love to see you fart like that in front of the doc."

Lara continued to fart and laugh simultaneously.

Two knocks at the door interrupted their play.

"OK, stop," Lara said, trying to gain her composure.

Dr. Roman, a dapper man in his late sixties, wearing a blue button down tucked into khakis, entered the room and closed the door behind him. He had a cap of white hair and a suspicious looking tan in the deep winter. "Having fun, kids?" said Dr. Roman.

"Is gas more common during pregnancy, Doc?" Seth inquired seriously.

Lara burst into laughter with a couple more farts popping and mumbled an apology, her face a lovely shade of pink.

Seth and Lara seemed to really enjoy this. The doctor simply smirked and then answered, "Everyone, pregnant or not, has some gas. You may be surprised to learn that the average person produces between one and four pints of gas each day and passes gas about fourteen to twenty-three times a day."

"I think she just did that in about thirty seconds," Seth remarked.

"Once a woman becomes pregnant," continued the doctor, "she may find herself belching or passing gas a lot more than usual or having to unbutton her pants to relieve bloating."

"Ugh," said Lara as she shook her head. "How are you feeling?" He looked at her compassionately.

Although he directed his question to Lara, Seth answered, "I'm all right now, Doc. Did my part, which was rather easy," he confided. "Ball's in Lara's court."

"Right." The doctor rolled his eyes. "As you move into the second trimester, you'll have to urinate more frequently."

"Buy wee-wee pads," Seth said aloud, making imaginary notes.

"Drink plenty of water. Don't dehydrate. Your ankles may swell up. If they get too big, call me."

"Tell me some good news," Lara quipped. "Baby boy in six months, is that good enough?" Seth asked.

"Let's take a look. It may be early, but I might see something. Do you want to know the sex?" Dr. Roman readied the ultrasound wand.

Lara took a long, considering look at Seth as she lay down on the exam table. "No, I don't think so." She giggled as he squeezed jelly on her belly. "Is this going to hurt?"

Dr. Roman gave the camera a smirk, "In a few months."

"Everyone's a comedian," Lara remarked.

"So where are you, little one? Where… are…ah, there you are!"

A black, gray, and white image of a fetus bounced onto the screen. Lara cupped her hands over her mouth with joy. For once, Seth was speechless.

"Vitals. Good. Yup, huh, yup… looking good, Daddy and Mommy, are you ready for parenthood?" He gave a long look at Seth holding the camera over his shoulder. "Well, I mean are you getting ready for the infestation?"

"Doc, our boy may look like a termite, but c'mon.

I saw pictures of your kids too," Seth replied laconically.

Dr. Roman's eyes never left the monitor as he retorted, "I don't see a termite here. Beautiful little…well, let's just say baby. I am, however, concerned about the cicada infestation."

"Is there a vaccination for that?"

"Seth!" Lara admonished. "Be serious." To the doctor she said, "Do you think it's a problem?"

The doctor removed the wand from Lara's belly.

"Yes. Hope for the best, but prepare for the worst. I'll admit that I am getting nervous with all the hype."

"You won't leave town?" Lara questioned. She was getting anxious herself.

"Lara, I delivered you. I'd never leave until I know our little one here is safe." He patted her tummy.

"Thank you, Dr. Roman." Lara sat up and put her arms out for a hug. "That's why I insisted on you for my delivery."

"Look, Seth. I don't want to cross hairs with you, but Lara's due around the emergence time. You should have a prep list."

"Do you?" Seth asked rudely to the doctor. "No, not really, but I don't have a pregnant wife." He slapped Lara's knee. "Enjoy your last few months of freedom."

* * *

Seth was speeding home. He was seething behind the wheel. This time, Lara filmed him.

"So... what do you think?" she asked tentatively. "About what?"

"The cicadas, Seth. What are you going to do?"

"Do? Are you nuts? It's just a way to generate income for the stores. How long are we really ever snowed in? Yet people strip the stores of all the processed food they can eat."

Lara knew he was right, but the cicada warning came from two credible sources: the news and her doctor. This didn't seem like a standard northeastern snowstorm.

"Oh, hurricane's coming," Seth dripped with sarcasm. "It's just a three-hour storm. It's over before it starts."

"Tell that to…"

"Aren't you breastfeeding anyway? They don't sell that in any store I know."

"You're still not convinced?"

"Nope. They are whipping people into a psycho frenzy. I laugh at the whole situation. Only an imbecile would take it seriously." "But the news said…"

"Jeez, Lara, you are so gullible. I've got this really nice bridge I'd like you to look at."

Even in his condescending tone, Lara still didn't know what to think. Stay with her husband's ideology and not prepare, or let this so-called emergency create a panic that may never even come. The air was as frigid in the car as in the winter landscape outside.

There was silence in the car while they drove back home. Seth was ruminating. Lara never had to work for anything in her life. Everything came easy to her. Her mom was at her beck and call growing up. Her older brothers were perfect princes. One became a doctor, the other a lawyer. She got good grades, was head of the cheerleading squad in high school, and was president of Alpha Epsilon Phi in college. All Lara ever had to do was show up, and everything else fell neatly into place for her. Seth was the first person she ever had to work for.

Seth took his eyes off the road and pointed to her. "You know what's going to happen when the 'cee-ca-das' arrive?

Nothing! They've been here for millions of years and will be coming back a million more."

Lara was still trying to come up with any excuse she could in hopes of convincing Seth to join the masses in preparing.

"We can at least stock up on some extra food," said Lara.

"So you're going from eating for two to eating for three?"

Whoops, the minute the words left his mouth, Seth regretted them.

"What?" Lara asked incredulously. "Nothing," said Seth as he slowly pulled into their driveway.

"What did you say?"

"Nothing. It was a joke gone bad." His green eyes caressed her while he put the car in park. "You know I love you and think you're the greatest thing that ever happened to me. I would never dream of having anyone else as my baby's mama."

She was annoyed with the food comment, but Lara couldn't hold a grudge. Seth had made snide remarks so many times in the past that she was seriously immune to them. But there was no way she was letting him off that easy. She liked to torture him a little. It was her duty, especially when he was being an asshole.

He started rubbing her knee as a peace offering. "Look." He nodded to their neighbor's house as he pulled into their driveway. "Crazy Jimmy's been prepping for years for the end of the world. I'll ask him for some pointers."

Lara turned toward him, unsure if he was just screwing with her.

"Happy?" asked Seth.

Lara knew the tone Seth used when he was serious. This time he wasn't joking.

"All I wanted you to do is to take some responsibility," she said softly.

"I know." He waggled his eyebrows. "That's why we made Valentino together."

"I love you, Seth," Lara added with a sigh. She did, she really did.

Seth leaned in and pecked her on the lips. Their fights never lasted for more than ten minutes. It was always better for her when he was on the defensive.

"We're getting close to Z again. Do we really have to start the alphabet over?"

"We do until we find a name we agree on. Look at that paddleboat. That Jimmy." They both eyed the paddleboat parked in the long driveway of their neighbor's home. "You know he bought that in case Long Island sinks."

"Just see if he has any news about Brood Ten. He must know something from all his prepping."

"Fine. Give me the camera, and I'll document what that nut job knows about the cicada doomsday. We'll see if he's been notified from the aliens that visit him."

*　*　*

Seth stomped over to the junkyard next door. There was a crude sign that said, "Keep Out—I'm Locked and Loaded." Seth noted the sign and sighed, "In more ways than one."

Even though they lived in a very affluent neighborhood, this was the one public eyesore, a rundown ranch with overgrown weeds and trees. A broken lamppost with twinkling Christmas lights interspersed with barbed wire was the only decoration on the outside of the house.

No one knew if Jimmy was sacrificing cats. But the fact remained his father was a large landowner in Muttontown, the neighboring affluent village, and the unofficial mayor of the surrounding towns. If you wanted something done, he knew whom to hire. Jimmy had clout, and he didn't give a rat's ass what people thought about him.

It didn't matter the season, there were always piles of decaying pine needles and brown leaves covering the lawn. The grass was overgrown. It was a jungle, by far the creepiest house in the neighborhood. The irony was that Jimmy was a landscaper by trade and a good one at that. He made damn sure whoever hired his services was going to get a beautiful, manicured lawn. However, when it came time to taking care of his own turf, Jimmy wasn't interested.

Ever the conspiracy theorist, he believed in all the kooky news that had plagued the human existence for centuries. The Bermuda Triangle, the grassy knoll, Area 51… Jimmy knew it all and he believed it too.

His most well known conspiracy was the flu shot. He thought the CDC was injecting transmitters into each subject so they would be able to track them everywhere.

He hated the "TV government." He knew deep down in his heart that there was a ruling elite run by Black Ops controlling everything. And of course he knew someone who worked for this "secret" government.

There were several cars of indeterminate colors parked in the gravel driveway, really in a state of sad disrepair. Bushes were neglected and snagged at Seth's fleece. He heard a litter of kittens meowing pitifully and muttered, "I should call and put this guy out of his misery."

Seth moseyed to the open garage where he heard clanging. There were carcasses of broken electronics visibly cannibalized for their many parts. The place stank, of what Seth could only guess. He noticed a nice patch of marijuana growing in a pot in a small corner of the garage and chuckled, "Maybe not such a bad neighbor after all. Have to think up some sort of trade. Let's see, Travis Bickle over here could sure use some of Lara's homemade artichoke dip. A fair and reasonable trade."

"What are you doing here?" Jimmy said louder than he should, bent over on one knee. Jimmy's unsightly ass crack filled Seth's vision. "You really should get a belt, Jim."

"What? What did you say?" Without turning around, Jimmy held out a smoking joint, ever the amicable host.

"Don't mind if I do." Seth took a toke and wondered when Lara kissed him later, would she know he and Jimmy shared more than a story about prepping?

Jimmy stood up and turned around holding a very large shotgun. He was a tall guy with cold slate eyes and a thick auburn beard that rested on his chest. His spindly legs looked too frail to hold his heavy upper torso. However thin his legs were, his arms were tree trunks with ham-fisted hands. He had thick sausage-like fingers that had a certain delicacy that belied their large size.

"You gotta be kidding me." Seth backed away unnerved. He briefly wondered if he stepped out of Oyster Bay and onto the set of. "Is that real?"

"Damn straight."

"Do we need the gun, Jimmy?"

"Not for you. One of my guys threatened me after I fired his lazy ass. Gotta make sure good ole Bess is cleaned." He rested the gun against a light blue fender. "How's Lucy?"

Seth didn't know who he was talking about. He wasn't sure if Lucy was a client of Jimmy's that Seth was supposed to know. Racking his brain, he came up with nothing, until it finally clicked.

"You mean Lara?"

"What?" Jimmy scratched his head. "Lucy's fine."

Jimmy moved to his filthy workbench. His gut was round and swollen. Guess Jimmy missed the memo about fatty liver disease, considering the fact he hadn't been to a doctor since high school.

"I am so getting ready for this," Jimmy explained.

"For what?"

"What's the matter with you?" Jimmy said over his shoulder. "Haven't you heard? They're coming! We have to be ready."

"What? The in-laws?"

"The infestation! You live under a rock?"

Jimmy swung around with a machete that was bigger than his arm. "You want something to eat?"

Seth thought he was going to hack off a kitten's head and offer it to him. As he would politely decline, Jimmy would probably drink the kitten's blood.

Jimmy yanked a piece of jerky from his pocket. "It's delicious. Try it."

Seth zoomed in on the linty piece of dry meat.

"Jimmy, it's full of shit from your pocket."

"So," he wagged the meat in front of the lens. "Let me tell you something, Seth. When you're hungry, anything will be good enough. I should shoot you just for filming in here, but you know what, it'll be good to have our stories documented."

He picked at the meat between his teeth with a dirty fingernail. "Those scientists have it all wrong."

"I knew it!" said a relieved Seth. "I absolutely knew it! I had a feeling all of this was hype."

"It's not millions of bugs."

"Of course not! What idiot came up with that bullshit?"

"It's gonna be trillions," Jimmy said slowly. Seth didn't believe it.

"Trillions?" asked Seth, waiting for the punch line. He was hoping a camera crew would jump from Jimmy's side door and say, "Surprise!"

"Trillions of those parasites messing with our infrastructure."

Seth wondered briefly how Jimmy knew a word that big. He probably read a lot in between his busy schedule.

"Rolling power outages, no deliveries, no trucking, all transportation will be at a standstill. No type of services anywhere. Civilization as we know it will be stopped. Kaput. Gone. Finished."

"Stop," Seth held up his hand. "I get it."

He paused and considered the very blue sky. "Yep. No ball games either."

"Well, in that case, it's clearly going to be a problem," Seth replied. "The good news is that at least it looks like the Mets can blame cicadas for their losing streak."

Jimmy threw the machete against the wall where it quivered stuck in the wood. He sighed with satisfaction and wiped his hands down his dirty jeans. Curling his finger, he urged Seth to come closer. "Look," he confided, "I got a buddy in the CIA." He looked furtively around to make sure they were completely alone. "He told me they did an evaluation of the soil in Pennsylvania, Connecticut, Jersey, Upstate New York and Long Island. There are trillions of them."

"Trillions?"

"Upon trillions and trillions."

"Did he tell you who killed Kennedy too?"

"He told me it's gonna be a big… fuckin'… mess."

Seth considered this for a minute. He went back to thinking if Jimmy took care of his place better, just maybe he might have believed him. Looking around the armpit he called a garage, Seth figured this guy was as crazy as the media.

"So, Jim, you got any cicada repellant? I'm looking for the environmentally friendly kind. Lucy thinks going green will make a difference with the ozone."

"You mean cicada killer?" "Sure."

Jimmy laughed, revealing very bad orthodontic work. Seth couldn't believe the guy would show his teeth like that.

Really, what were his parents thinking? This was Oyster Bay, after all. No wonder he never had a date, Seth thought.

"You can't kill something of this magnitude with fairy dust. World's ending. Better move fast. Here, take some batteries and flashlights." Jimmy pressed a flashlight into Seth's hand.

"I didn't come here for flashlights, dude. I have batteries at home," Seth told him.

"Have you tested them? Do you know if they even work?"

"Um, I have to ask Lucy."

Jimmy looked disgusted with this poor excuse of a man. "Pussy."

Seth was about to blurt out when was the last time Jimmy got laid, but he caught sight of the pistol grip pump action 12-gauge again. Better he kept his mouth shut.

"Take this box." He reached up and grabbed a box from a large stack in the corner and wiped off a layer of mouse crap. Seth wondered briefly if he was going to get the Hantavirus.

"Is it fairy dust?" Seth asked hopefully.

"I don't know why, but I like you," Jimmy laughed.

"Well, that's a relief," Seth said with a sigh.

"It's water in plastic packets," Jimmy explained. "Thanks, Jimmy, but our water's fine. Lara, I, uh, mean Lucy won't drink from plastic." This time he leaned closer to confide.

"She thinks it causes cancer."

"Listen. Once they get into the water system, it's finished. Just take it. Stack up on canned goods."

"She has a problem with lead in the cans," Seth shared.

"Well, neighbor, tell her to get over it." "Jimmay… Jimmay…" The strident call came from the house. "Who are you talking to?"

Jimmy rolled his eyes. "I'm with the neighbor, Ma. Whatya want?"

A beast of a woman lumbered into view.

Wearing a faded pink housedress, hair piled in an untidy bun, Jimmy's mother stood in the doorway in filthy bunny slippers.

"Oh hey, are you Lucy's husband?"

"Yup. How are you, Mrs. Cain? Nice day today." Seth smiled.

"Damn mice in the house. Jimmy, put out that poison I told you was in the garage. I don't want to get no Hantavirus," she harrumphed and blew through a pursed mouth.

"Can you really get the Hantavirus by breathing in mouse crap?" Seth inquired a little nervously.

"Jimmy been talking to you about the infestation?" the mother interrupted.

"Of mice?"

"Cicada!" she shouted. "Yes, ma'am."

"You got weapons?"

"Weapons, um, no. No, I don't like guns." "When's baby coming?" she demanded.

Seth didn't know what the hell was going on or what the hell they were talking about. He actually had to think for a minute; the conversation was all over the map. "Late August."

"Better get prepared, boy. Jimmy, give him a knife. He

don't like guns, so give him your knife." Ma Cain pointed to Jimmy's back pocket.

"Aw, Mom, I love this knife," Jimmy whined. "I said give it to him." She looked at him with laser eyes in her sweaty red face.

Seth shuddered, wondering briefly what was going on in this loony bin. "Jimmy!" she yelled, looking at her son with an expression that boded ill.

"Dammit," he muttered under his breath, taking out his lethal-looking pocketknife and handing it to Seth.

"Well," Seth said, taking it with his thumb and forefinger, "that's not a Boy Scout knife."

"Tell me about it."

"Thanks, Jimmy. You're a good man." Seth liked him for all his craziness. "Thanks, Mrs. Cain. I'll give your regards to m'wife." He smiled at her.

"It's just been sharpened. Can cut through anything," Jimmy warned him. "Here take some duct tape too." Jimmy tossed him a gray roll of duct tape. "That stuff's good for everything." Seth deftly caught it.

"When all this begins, come over for pizza. We'll have a cicada doomsday party," Seth said as he retreated.

* * *

Seth wore old faded jeans slung low over his waist. He knew he looked good and it seemed a shame to waste his look on hard labor. Three paint cans lay unopened on the floor. Cursing, he picked them up, put them in the hallway and unfolded a spotted drop cloth over the new carpet.

He placed his rollers, sponges, and tape in a neat pile in the center of the room. Popping open the lid, he stirred the ice blue color and pondered if he should scrape the windows more. That was a bitch and he hated painting. If he was working, they would have hired a handyman, but under the circumstances, it seemed uneconomical.

Well, he thought grimly, it looked easy enough on television and he wanted to get the job done, before Lara came from school. She wasn't expecting this and boy would she be surprised. She was mad as hell when he managed to score extra batteries for the camcorder, but nothing for the flashlights.

Seriously pissed, he could hear her little brain wondering what he was doing all day. Well, he sighed, he did try. There were no batteries around, anywhere. But, he figured, they had time until the emergence. He could pick them up next month.

Maybe he'd tell her father to send them from Arizona. On second thought, hell no. There wasn't a thing super dad couldn't do. Seth would get the batteries, he knew he would, but now he had to work on getting the room painted.

Working in silence, he never realized two hours had passed. It really wasn't such a terrible job.

Spreading the paint had a soothing effect and gave him time to think. His job on Wall Street had evaporated in the credit crisis. It's not that he even loved the job, he was not an aggressive broker, but his personality brought him sales. He actually felt that he was selling nothing and it seemed unethical, like he was a con man. He didn't mind that fact that the job ended. He really didn't know what he wanted to do. It was depressing when you think that you go to school and when you get out you are sentenced to work for the rest of your life. Shouldn't work be fun? He wished for a minute he had a talent or a passion for something. Well, he liked to eat. That was something, he shrugged. Maybe he should do something involving food. He considered the possibilities and didn't hear his wife creep up into the room.

"Oh, it's so nice," she exclaimed startlingly him. He jumped hitting the white ceiling with the blue colored roller.

"Crap. I'll have to fix that." he thought, looking up.

"You did such a good job. It's a great color." "Yeah," he sat down wearily on the floor. Patting the floor, Lara obliged and sank down next to him. "Tired?"

"Yes, but in a good way. Maybe I'll try to get a job painting."

Lara considered his amateurish job and didn't have the heart to tell him that it probably wasn't a very good idea.

"Hungry?" she asked.

"Starved. I forgot to eat lunch."

Lara looked at him, he was strangely subdued. "You okay?"

"Never better. You in the mood for peanut butter and jelly?"

"Yummm."

* * *

"Let's go for a walk," Lara asked eagerly while she put on her winter coat.

"It's freezing outside." Seth complained.

"I don't care. It smells like snow and I just want to get some air."

Seth shrugged into his parka and they strolled arm in arm down the quiet street.

"I love this place," Lara said dreamily. "It's the perfect neighborhood to bring up kids. I'm so happy we moved here."

"Any place where you are is the perfect place,"

Seth kissed the top of her head. "How was school?" "I had a ball today. The kids are delightful. We are studying butterflies. I read somewhere I can buy a kit and sort of grow them. I'm thinking of doing it this spring. '

"That ought to be fun. Are you going to be okay with insects in the classroom? It's cold, Lara. I don't think this was such a good idea."

"Indulge me. Let's walk faster. It'll keep us warm."

"I can think of a better way to keep you warm. " "Race you home," she smiled mischievously at him and they made it home in record time.

CHAPTER 4
HIBERNATION

"Perhaps I am a bear, or some hibernating animal underneath, for the instinct to be half asleep all winter is so strong to me."

- Anne Morrow Lindbergh

LARA SNATCHED THE charging camcorder from the kitchen counter calling out, "Come on Seth! Don't take all day."

She made her way to the car parked in the garage. Making a nest for herself inside the car with her list, water, oversized purse and of course the ever-present camcorder, she watched the minutes on the dash ticking by and rolled her eyes impatiently. With the palm of her hand, she pressed the horn wincing at its loud blare. "That man!" she muttered.

Another five minutes passed and she angrily yanked open the car door as Seth skipped out of the garage entrance.

"Miss me?" he crooned.

"What took you so long?" her mouth narrowed to a firm line.

"Don't do that," Seth warned. "You look like your mother."

While Lara busied herself digging out trail mix from her mammoth bag, Seth pulled out of the driveway, into the early springtime.

The leaves started budding with that fresh light green color. The air was soft with the smell of jasmine.

"Open the sunroof, Seth. Do you smell those flowers?" Lara asked taking a deep breath.

"Yeah, my allergies are killing me. What's the plan ma'am?"

"The baby store. The baby furniture store. The toy store. But I need some decaf coffee," Lara said.

"I'm your chauffeur and I will take you wherever your little heart desires."

"And don't forget," Lara interrupted. "Jimmy said we should stock up on batteries. Do you want to do that first?"

"Nah, we could pick 'em up on the way back. I also need new netting for the hoop."

"Oh, right, and I want new stationary," she remembered adding another item to her list.

*　*　*

Lara filmed Seth coming out empty-handed from yet another store.

"What happened?" she called out.

"They were all out of batteries," Seth entered the car. "No worries, babe. I'll try somewhere else tomorrow."

"Seth."

"What?"

"What do you mean they were all out?"

"I cannot be any more specific," Seth deadpanned. "Do you want to go in?"

"Not really."

"So, like I said, I'll find some tomorrow. It's no big deal. We'll get it when more shipments arrive."

"I don't believe this. That's four stores. Where are all the batteries?"

"Are we done yet?" Seth asked with a long- suffering sigh.

"I really have to get that stationary. We need it. One more stop."

Seth slouched his shoulders and drove to the next outlet.

*　*　*

Lara entered the car carrying loose papers in her hand.

"Do you want to see my stationary?" she asked. "It's so pretty."

"No," Seth said unhappily. "I want to go eat."

"You promised to be my chauffeur today. We're not done yet," Lara looked up to him, her blue eyes wide with excitement.

"That was then, this is now. And five stops later, really Lara, I've had enough. I want to go eat."

They drove off to the diner.

* * *

There was nothing Seth liked better than food shopping and he was going to film the experience to show Lara when he got home. Usually Lara did all the shopping, but lately, she had been too tired. He volunteered happily, racing his cart up and down the aisles. Fruits and vegetables were never his forte. Somehow, she complained his pears were too soft and the melons too hard. That doesn't sound promising, he smirked. He noticed a new display being set up, much like the supermarkets did as a holiday approached. He wondered if he was forgetting some upcoming event. Strolling towards it, his cart smacked into another one.

"Hey Seth, what's new?"

It was Cathy, their neighbor from across the street.

"Nothing much, food shopping. Helping Lara."

She talked to him, but was eyeing the workers setting up the new display. "What's that all about?"

"I don't know. I was just about to check it out myself." With their shopping carts, they walked side by side to the rows of food being set up. There were huge cans, vegetables, fruit, shortening, all in super jumbo sized. Two men were loading them on the shelf.

"What's going on?" asked Seth.

An overweight, balding man wearing a dirty white coat, wiped the sweaty forehead and walked over to them. "Our store is participating in the new 'Ready, Set, Go' program."

"What's that?' Cathy asked as he handed her a flyer.

"We are taking responsibility by urging people to stock

up and be prepared for the upcoming cicada event this summer. These canned goods are approved."

"User approved? What kind of shit…" Seth started to ask.

"Shush, Seth. What does that mean?" Cathy interrupted him. She had already started loading cans of string beans and carrots into her cart. They were mammoth sized.

"United States Emergency Rations, its run by the CER?"

"And what pray tell, is the CER?" Seth inquired looking at a super-sized bag of potato chips. Now this, he was going to need.

"Central Emergency Rationing. It's the new organization that the government set up for when there are shortages. Here," he handed Seth a pamphlet. "This is what they suggest you have in the house."

Seth scanned the list. Cathy grabbed one from the man and started loading up canned gallon-sized peas.

"No thanks," Seth gave back the paper. "How bad could it get?" The only thing he planned to stock up on was dip to go with his chips. He waved to Cathy who now was stuffing freeze dried turkey onto the bottom of her cart, "Bye, Cath. Don't forget to get dog food."

"Oh my God," she cried out, "Where is the emergency supply for pets?"

Seth heard her panicked cries as he strolled the beverage section for a six pack grinning.

*　*　*

Seth grabbed the camcorder and his baseball cap and headed for the garage.

"I'll be back in an hour," he called out to Lara. "I'm going to the hardware store."

Pulling the car out of the garage, he paused to look at his forsythia bush and mentally noted to get rope to tie it back together. The heavy snow had crushed and broken the bush, and now that its bright yellow buds were blooming, he could see if he didn't tie it up, the bush would die.

There was a lot of activity on his quiet street. People were out, bringing bulky boxes into their houses. "Well, this is encouraging," he thought. Maybe it would jolt the sagging economy. Perhaps a job would turn up.

The normally quiet streets of Oyster Bay were packed with springtime shoppers. Cars were double- and triple-parked. Local stores were doing a booming business. Seth reflected, if this was any sign, it looked like things were bouncing back. That should please the wife.

He pulled into a small hardware store off the main street of town. He liked it better than the big- box stores; he got more personal attention there.

There was a line out the door. Squeezing in, he looked for a familiar face. It was bedlam. He held up a hand and tried to get the attention of the store's owner. "Rich?" he called out. "Richie." Richard, the owner, glanced at Seth.

"I don't have time, Seth," he called out from behind the counter. The phones were ringing off the hook. "It's packed."

"What's going on?" Seth shouted over the din. "What do you think? The cicadas," Richard shrugged. "Batteries, generators, you name it. Listen, bro, I can't take you out of place. Get in line."

Seth shook his head. "Nah. I'll come back."

Seth strode out of the store, without rope or batteries for that matter. He would get to it later, he thought.

Maybe he'd try online.

Seth left the store and eased into his car. He dropped the camera on the passenger seat pointing directly at him. Flipping on the radio, he scanned the stations. was blasting on Long Island's best News Talk.

Seth loved Bobby the shock jock. He had an acerbic wit and a sarcastic slant that mirrored Seth's own opinions.

"Bugs, shmugs!" Bobby quipped. "Hey Michelle, what are you doing to prep for this? Did you build a bug bunker yet? Everyone is bugging out and going buggers!"

Michelle, the sidekick, her voice a throaty hum, responded, "I'm scared of spiders! I hate them!"

"My sentiment exactly." Bobby responded. "If it was spiders that were attacking Long Island, now that would be a problem. And wasn't there a movie about spiders attacking a small town some time ago? Spiders are scary, I'll give you that. But cicada? C'mon! Don't they die after a few days or something? Can't they come up with something more terrifying than a harmless little cicada?

What's next, a mutant ladybug litter? A praying mantis mother load?"

Michelle cannot stop giggling at Bobby's bug rant. Even Seth found it amusing.

"A tsetse fly tumult?"

"A mosquito mosh?" Michelle added.

"Exactly! Oh, looks like we got a caller. We have Ryan from Oceanside. Ryan, how the hell are ya?"

"Doing great, Bobby. Long time listener. Love the show."

"Thank you, Ryan. What's on your mind? What do you think about this bugabaloo?"

Clearly educated, Ryan spoke, "Look guys, I'm taking this thing a little more seriously this week. The stores are ."

"What?!" Bobby cackled. "This is media generated hysteria. So the big box stores and the food marts will move all the old junk they've accumulated. I don't believe any of this for a minute."

Seth pumped his fist and pointed his finger at the radio. "My man Bobby! Love ya baby!"

"But Bobby," Ryan continued. "I can't find batteries anywhere. Do you remember the gas shortages…?"

Bobby the host interrupted, "Oh come on you twerp, what could these bugs possibly do? They are bugs! B. U. G. S. Bugs! Don't tell me, Ryan, you're drinking the media driven Kool-Aid. You're gonna make those corporations rich. Next caller. We have Marilyn from Woodbury. Marilyn, you're on with Bobby and Michelle live. Talk to me baby, what's on your mind."

"Get outta here with this bug junk. These people are nuts. This has never happened before, and they're making a big deal about a bunch of insects."

Bobby interrupted, "Hold on, honey, I'm gonna three-way a call."

"Hello?" a distant voice said.

"You're on with Bobby, Michelle, and Marilyn."

"This is Connie. I live in Dix Hills," a timid voice said over the airways.

"Well hello Connie from Dix Hills. What do you think about the Great Cicada Invasion? Please speak up. We can barely hear you."

"My husband and I, along with our Church, are taking this very seriously. I mean, like, there were bug plagues in the Bible, you know, in Exodus. It could really happen here."

"C'mon Connie," Bobby cut her off. "They have something called pesticides. It's the twenty first century."

Michelle started laughing at Bobby's comments and replied, "Maybe Bobby, you should go part the water in the Long Island Sound. Use your special staff."

Everyone on the radio, except for Connie, found this amusing.

Seth flipped off the radio as he pulled into his driveway. He figured he would go look on the web for some batteries.

The forsythia bush drooped unhappily as he walked past it. He decided he would surf the net for rope too.

Unfortunately, upon entering the house, he got distracted by the half open bag of chips laying on the counter. Throwing himself down on the couch, chips and beer, he lazed the rest of the afternoon in a salty coma of satisfaction.

* * *

"Put the camera away, please, Seth," Lara implored him from the couch.

"Lar, this is our story, our. He-he." "Cut it out; this is important," she replied patiently as if talking to a child.

Seth laid the camcorder on the side table. "What's up?"

Lara took his hand and gently played with his fingers.

"You know when you do that, Lar, I find it hard to concentrate."

Lara threw his hands away with disgust. "Listen, something weird is going on. I went to the market today. The shelves are empty. Empty. None of the groceries I get were there. They don't know when to expect them. There was plenty of cat food though."

"We don't have a cat."

"Exactly! That's what I'm saying. The things I use were not in stock."

"Go to another store then," Seth shrugged. "I did. They were out too. I also went to our butcher. He told me to stock up. Seth, let's buy another freezer."

"Lara, we just don't have the money to buy another stupid appliance."

"I can ask my parents…"

"No, no, and no. Did I say no? I don't want anything else from your parents. I promise you, they are just stimulating the economy. This isn't going to be a problem. I will get you whatever you need," Seth hugged her. "Have I ever let you down?"

Lara kissed him gently on the lips. "I love you so much, but I think we need the freezer," she persisted.

"Is it going to make you happy?" Seth sighed. "Yessss," Lara smiled at this small victory.

"OK, let's get a freezer."

* * *

"Can you get that?" Lara yelled from the basement. The doorbell rang again.

"Seth!" she shouted. "I'm doing laundry. Get the door." Lara called impatiently from the basement steps. "I can't do those steps again. Seth!"

"Keep your pants on," Seth shouted back.

Seth put the camcorder down on the kitchen table where he was inspecting it. The doorbell chimed again, but before Lara could scream, Seth called out "I got it," and walked over to the door.

"Jimmy my man," Seth was surprised to see his neighbor on the front door step and held open the door for him to enter.

"I'm all dirty," Jimmy motioned to his soiled jeans. "Wanna come over to my place?"

Seth shook his head no. "Can't leave Lara. She's in the basement. I'll meet you in the backyard. Do you want a beer?"

"Sure," replied Jimmy. "You got a Bud?" "Heineken?"

"Well, if that's all you got."

"I may have a Samuel Adams Summer Ale…" "Sisssy stuff, I'll take the Heineken."

Jimmy headed into the back, trailing all kinds of dirt and humus in his wake. After grabbing the beer and camcorder, Seth stepped into the late morning sunshine. Dropping the items on this picnic table, Seth opened the oversized orange-cantilevered umbrella. They had bought it at the end of the season last year. It covered the entire patio and brought much needed shade to the late spring day. The beers sweated on the table.

Taking out a filthy terry towel, Jimmy smeared the dirt on his face. After a long swig he sighed, "Man, not bad. I prefer the American beers. Bud, Coors, you know. This isn't half bad."

"Yeah, me too," Seth replied. "What can I do ya for Jim?"

"My Ma," Jimmy said. "She sent this book over for the Missus. He pulled a dog-eared paperback from his back pocket, handing it to Seth.

"Home Deliveries," Seth read the title. "I don't think they're talking about Chinese food."

"Ha!" Jimmy exploded. "You're funny, Seth.

Nah, it's my mom's book on how to deliver a baby at home. My mom wanted your wife to have it."

"Sort of Childbirth for Dummies?" "Well I guess, my mom is a doula." "A what?" Seth choked on his beer.

"A doo-lah," Jimmy said slowly. "When she used to leave the house, she helped women give birth."

"She doesn't leave the house? What happened?" "Well, after my dad died, she started eating and couldn't stop. She was beautiful when she was young. Then when she put on, I don't know, about two hundred pounds, she stopped leaving the house. She can barely walk anymore. Can't fit in the electric wheelchair I bought her either. Lucky thing I live in a ranch." Jimmy shrugged, his eyes filled. "She was something else when she was young, an asset to the community. As the old neighbors moved out, the new ones don't want to bother with her, except for your wife. She's a nice girl."

As if on cue, Lara looked out on them from the sliding doors, holding a basket filled with folded laundry. "Hi, Jimmy. How's your mom? I bought some of that relish she liked last week. Make sure you take it home."

Jimmy jumped to his feet. "Can I help you with that, Mrs. Fletcher."

Lara laughed. "I told you to call me Lara, Jimmy."

Jimmy's face turned beat red to the tips of his ears.

Seth got up and took the laundry from a surprised Lara. Nobody was going to outshine him with manners. "Thanks Jimmy, I got it," Seth said.

Lara's mouth formed a perfect "O" then followed with a sweet smile of satisfaction. "Thanks hon," she winked at him.

"Jimmy's mother sent over some reading material for us." He gestured the book with a nod.

Lara stepped outside and took a seat in the shade. She kicked off her shoes and tucked her feet underneath her. "It's hot for April I don't get it. It was so cold, and then it's like the heat got turned on. The weather has been so weird." She picked up the book and smiled, "Tell your mom thank you.

She's so sweet to think of me."

"Our pleasure ma'am," Jimmy laughed with delight.

Seth set the laundry basket on the kitchen table so he could go back outside. He usually didn't mind Jimmy, but this was a peculiar side of his neighbor he never saw before.

Jimmy stood, "Well I gotta go. Make sure you stock up before the, you know." He looked at Seth. He picked up his empty beer bottle and looked at them questionably where to put it.

"Oh, don't worry," Lara reassured him. "We recycle."

After he left, Seth and Lara exchanged looks followed with a chuckle.

"He brought homework. Childbirth 101," Seth informed her. "It may be useful."

Lara flipped through the pages and made a face.

Seth took the book and threw it across the table. "Seth!" Lara reached for it.

"I think our neighbor has a crush on you," Seth shared.

"Don't be silly. Look at me," she gestured her burgeoning waist.

"I don't think you've ever been lovelier."

"Oh Seth," Lara sat on his lap and kissed his lips. "Am I too heavy?"

Seth adjusted her to fit in the cradle of his lap as his lips found hers and he whispered, "Never."

* * *

Lara sat at the kitchen counter, her head resting in her palm, her face pensive. A small television was droning on about news of the upcoming cicada invasion, making her both unsettled and a bit nervous.

She was flipping through the illustrated pages of the childbirth book.

"Hey baby, whatcha doing?" the camcorder was filming her.

"Stop," she pushed Seth away. "You should be watching this."

Seth put the camcorder on the stool, "What? Oh cicada again?"

He went to shut the TV and Lara stayed his hand. "Really stop," she was annoyed. "You should know what we have to do."

"Did you talk to your parents today?" Seth asked, an idea forming in his head.

Lara ignored him, her eyes glued to the program. Seth stormed out of the room with a curse.

Lara sighed, shut the TV and went downstairs to do a laundry. For some reason, laundry duties always calmed her. Seth returned ready to make peace, only to find an empty kitchen. The book's pages ruffled in the breeze from the open screen door. Grabbing a jar of peanuts, he sat munching and drew the book closer to him.

Seth put the nuts down and read the first page aloud, "Be prepared," he paused, furrowed his brow and said, "Duh. Let's see what else this font of wisdom has to offer."

He learned that you're supposed to dial 9-1-1. "Well what a surprise," he muttered. "Stay calm? No shit." Seth almost put the book down, but after fanning through a few chapters the actual act of delivering a baby in an emergency caught his eye.

"Try a side-lying position…Positioning yourself on your side will also lessen the intensity of the contractions and diminish the pressure, which in turn will help to prevent the baby's head from popping out…if the head of the baby is presenting, it is best to push between contractions rather than at the height of the contraction. These methods will help prevent tearing."

Seth shuddered and said, "Ouch," he continued reading. "There is no need for manipulation of the shoulders unless more than three or four minutes has passed since the birth of the head…the umbilical cord will be clamped before it is cut with something to help seal off the open blood vessels in the cord…though it can also be a metal cord clamp or even cord tape. What is used depends largely on your practitioner…"

Seth put the book down and said, "I better know that route to the hospital."

* * *

Lara stood by the window, grimly watching some activity outside.

"What's new, baby doll?" Seth walked in and kissed the back of her neck.

"It's that damn dog again," she tapped on the window. "Stop that! Look," she cried out, near tears. "He's digging up my tulips!"

"Wait. I gotta get this on camera!" Seth ran for the camcorder.

"Stop!" she shouted. "Casey!" she called to the dog. "Stop. Oh, I'm going to get a broom and shove it up his…"

"Lara, calm down. I'll talk to Jeff about his dog. See," he showed her the camera. "I have proof."

Seth strolled out the front door, the spring sun warm on his face. Kids were out playing basketball. Sun heated the damp earth, and trees budded all around him. He paused to admire the crocus they'd planted poking through the rich soil and felt like landed gentry. He was Baron Fletcher of his domain. Growing up in a smoky apartment with his mom and her string of boyfriends, he breathed deep of the air of affluence. It was special here, God's country. He loved Long Island. When Lara landed her job locally, he agreed to the town. It was far from her parents, and his mom was also a plane trip away. He loved the isolation. People sometimes forget that Long Island is actually an island. It felt remote from the rest of the country, and Seth enjoyed that.

He sauntered across the green acres of suburbia and saw Jeff washing his car, Casey the dog lapping at the running streams of water happily.

"Hi, neighbor!"

"Hey, Seth. What do you think about the Mets?" "Can't hit for shit. Yanks man, myself," responded Seth.

"Go home, Yankee!" Jeff laughed. "How's Lara? What's the camera for?"

"Home movies of Casey digging up Lara's tulips," Seth laughed.

"Sorry." Jeff reached down and played with his dog's floppy ears. "He's a nuisance, but you gotta love him."

"I don't care, but she was ," Seth said with a smirk.

They both thought that was hilarious.

"You want me to send over the gardeners to fix it?"

"Nah. Just wave your arms a bit, so Lara thinks you're defensive." Jeff obliged him. "Yeah, great!" Seth pointed his finger aggressively and winked. "She's gonna love this."

Cathy, Jeff's wife, poked her head out the door. "Hi, Seth. Hear about the cicadas?"

Both men looked at each other and rolled their eyes.

"Here we go again," Jeff said.

"I know," responded Seth. Then he turned to Cathy and replied, "We bought a freezer for the basement," he shrugged, embarrassed. "Made Lara happy."

Cathy turned to her husband, "See, I told you. We need a freezer too."

"Cathy, we don't need a freezer. It's stupid."

"You're stupid," she pounded down the steps.

"Oops, my bad," Seth said sheepishly. "Sorry, man." He looked at Cathy approaching them like a Sherman tank. "I'm outta here."

"I wish I could be too," Jeff mourned and let the hose drop so he could finish his argument. Seth bounced back into his house smiling at Lara, who was watching the fight across the street.

"Told them a thing or two," Seth boasted.

* * *

The doorbell rang insistently. Once, twice, and then four more times. Seth raced up the basement steps to find his neighbor's daughter dressed up in a green uniform and looking up expectantly at him.

"Can I help you Emmy?"

"Hi Theth." Her lisp sent Seth into gales of laughter.

"Wath it thomething I thed?"

"No Emmy, but you sure are cute. Where are your front teeth?" Seth pointed to vacant spot in the front of her smile.

"Loth them. I am earning a badge on the thacadas." She held up a shoebox with wire hangers cut through the sides holding up netting. "Thith is a thacada catcher. If you buy one, I get poinths to my badge."

"Well then, we must buy one. In fact, I'll take two."

"I only have one." Poor Emmy looked downcast.

"One will do just fine. How much?" Seth asked. "Three dollarths."

"A steal. Wait here." Seth ran into the kitchen where his wallet lie on the counter. He slid out three bucks and went back to the door and gave it to the little girl.

"Pretty impressive." He rolled back the screen. "They get thuck in there. Then they die," Emmy informed him with relish.

"Good work. Do you have cookies for sale too?" Seth asked hopefully.

"Cookies are nexth month. Thanks Theth. Bye." Emmy let the screen door slam on Seth's knee and he hopped back into the house holding his cicada trap. "This will impress Lara. Wait till I tell her father I got traps," he laughed.

* * *

"Do you know what you look like?" Seth laughed and ran for the camcorder to document his wife. "I swear, the angels sang when you were born, Lara. You look like Snow White."

She touched her belly and wrinkled her pert nose, "I don't remember Snow White sporting a baby bump. Those are always missing from the Fairy Tales."

Seth shouted with laughter. "Okay, but what are you doing with the salad?"

"Salad?" Lara looked down at the Tupperware she was holding. "It's just greens, well, carrots and lettuce to be specific. I haven't seen any bunnies this year. You remember the pair that used to come here last spring."

"Yeah, Bunny and Clyde." He paused for a minute. "You know you're right. I never noticed." Seth took the basket and started going towards the brambles, throwing the greens further than Lara could reach. "I wonder where the bunnies went," he murmured.

*　*　*

The camera was laying under the cantilever on the picnic table filming his DIY moment. Seth was underneath a weeping willow, humming from. He loved that movie. "Br'er Rabbit was such a character." He shook his head. His one great memory was when his mother and her then boyfriend Joe took him to Disneyland for a trip of a lifetime. He ate so much and went on every ride, afraid he would never go back again, that he threw up on Main Street during the parade. Even though it was humiliating, he never forgot the innocent joy of being a kid. He couldn't wait to take his own son on the same rides that exhilarated him as a small boy.

He had purchased a bird feeder two years ago, but never opened it. Today was the perfect day to fill it with the organic bird feed that Lara bought and hopefully it will turn his backyard into Disneyland.

It was a long thin tube with a heavy base. He attached a small twine and hung it on the tree. Backing off to admire his handiwork, he nodded with approval. It swayed gently, and fell emptying birdseed all over the grass.

Sighing, he picked it up and gave it another try. He heard Lara entering through the garage. By the time she dropped her bags and put her bottle of water in the refrigerator, he had successfully hung it from the tree and was singing lustily to draw her outside to see his creation.

"Oh, Seth! That is so cute!" an overjoyed Lara said as she emerged from the kitchen. "Good work! By the way, the crib is coming tomorrow. That should be a breeze."

"This took me like two hours!" "So?"

"I'll be finished with the crib by Christmas."

"As long as it's done by late August, I don't care how long it takes you."

* * *

The crib lay in pieces littering the floor of the light blue painted room.

"I'm not sure I like this color." Lara considered the walls.

"What's wrong with it. It's manly." Seth reached up to pull a piece of masking tape that still adhered to the trim.

"What are you going to do with all this?" Lara gestured the piles of hardware, surrounding the rails of a mahogany colored crib.

Sighing, Seth stretched up to scratch the back of his neck. "I'll get to it. It's just really confusing. I can't imagine what putting together his bicycle is going to be like."

"Do you think we should have paid for them to do it?"

"No. I said I would get to it. I mean, how hard could this really be?"

* * *

It was a hot June day and they both wanted to be by the pool. Seth and Lara drove down the street on the way for a nice brunch at the diner

"Man, it's quiet," Seth observed.

"I know. The fourth isn't for a few weeks. I thought school wasn't letting out early this year." Lara looked at the deserted homes. "People must have left for vacation early. I thought they were talking about keeping kids in the school until the end of June."

"Oh, you know the people here. They must have gone crazy that it would eat into vacation time.

They all take the kids somewhere before camp. Yeah, we'll squeeze in Europe before li'l Johnny starts basketball camp this year."

"Oh, you're so romantic, Seth," Lara said with a giggle. "I knew someday I'd get you to Europe."

Seth shuddered, "Anything to avoid going to Arizona and visiting Ozzie and Harriet."

Lara looked at him sideways. "Maybe we should go to San Francisco and join your mom on her groupie tour with Jimmy Buffett," she said, referring to Seth's mom and her Parrothead obsession.

"Nah, she's in the Keys this week." Seth didn't approve of his mom's pastimes. She could drink him under the table and made him feel like a rookie.

"Oh," Lara defended, "I like her free spirit." "Ugh," Seth drawled, "I'd rather go to

Uzbekistan than spend time with her."

"Well, maybe Paris," Lara offered. "But that still doesn't explain where everybody has gone."

They spied a neighbor loading his car, and Seth pulled over.

"Seth, what are you doing? We don't even know this guy."

"That's no problem. I'm the neighborly type. Hello," Seth called out from the driver's side of the car.

The man bent over and warily took in the both of them from the passenger side.

"Hi, I'm Seth. We live on Cheshire."

"Garrett. Garrett Basso." His arms were full, so he just nodded his head.

"Yeah, hi, Garrett. What's going on? The street looks deserted. You heading for Europe?"

"Europe? No." Garrett glanced at his wife shepherding two small boys from the house, several bags hanging on her arms.

"Garrett, you wanna give me a hand?" she shrieked.

"I'll be right there. Look, I got to go. We're outta here." He looked at Lara's protruding belly. "I got a place in the woods. Upstate. I need time to set up." "Set up what?" Seth asked.

"Ya know, the cicadas. I've got a wife and kids. I'm not taking any chances." He motioned to Lara. "You shouldn't either. Get out of town."

Lara gasped.

The wife yelled, "Garrett!"

"All right!" he screamed back and turned back to Seth. "Look, I don't have time to chat. Gotta load up the car."

As they pulled away, Lara turned to Seth. "Maybe we should go to my parents'?" Lara looked at him, her blue eyes wide and scared.

"In this case, I do know what's worse…your parents," Seth responded. "Everybody will be back in September and feeling foolish. And by the way, do you think they don't have bugs in the Catskills? In my opinion he's going from the frying pan into the fire. I wouldn't worry about it, Lar. Aside from that, if we change zip codes, you'd have to find a new doctor for Jesse."

"Jesse? We'll have to talk about that one," Lara responded with a smile.

* * *

The camera was charging on the kitchen counter. The front door swung open and Seth rushed into the house, slamming it behind him. Dripping with sweat, he was in expensive running gear.

He raced for the camcorder, and after wiping his face with a dishtowel, he positioned the camera so he could film his face. Flushed and disheveled, he chugged down a mini bottle of water in one gulp.

"Man that was weird," he said to no one in particular. Then he spoke to the lens of the camcorder.

"Hi, all. I want to document what happened. It was so…I can't describe…weird. I was jogging, you know. It's gorgeous outside. I heard planes, horns honking, but I did notice something strange, very strange. I want to know where all the birds have gone. I have a feeder."

He took the camera and focused on a bird feeder swaying in the summer breeze in their backyard. "I haven't replaced the food in weeks. Where are the birds?" The door opened and Lara entered carrying a shopping bag. He was momentarily distracted. "Oh hi, honey, what's for dinner?"

The camera went dark.

CHAPTER 5
COMPANY

"Staying with people consists in your not having your own way, and their not having theirs."

- Maarten Maartens

SETH HEARD A loud crash followed by an exasperated scream.

"Lara," he yelled jumping to his feet taking the steps from the basement two at a time. "Lara, answer me. Are you alright?!"

"I'm fine. Nothing happened," she answered in a distracted voice.

He bumped into the pantry wall separating the laundry room from a small pantry closet.

"What happened?" A huge box of salt lay broken on the floor. Lara bent to pick it up and Seth stayed her. "I'll do it. You should have called me if you wanted to get something from the top shelf."

He turned to get a dust shovel and whisk broom. "What a mess."

"You have no idea. Look! Ewww." She brushed a pile of the salt away revealing a colony of ants furiously working on taking whatever they could from the spill. "I don't know how they got in here."

Seth crouched down and wiped at the pile of salt. "This is disgusting. Make sure you call an exterminator on Monday. They are huge."

"I know. Maybe you should use the dust buster." "If I do, it's going into the garbage right after," Seth warned.

"I'm okay with that," Lara replied grimly.

*　*　*

Seth loosened his tie and fell into his easy chair with a sigh. This interview didn't even get off the ground. He had months of unemployment left, but it felt as though he was competing with more people for less opportunity. The doorbell screamed in the silence and he cursed, walked over and was shocked to see his brother-in-law standing in the entrance holding a beat up cardboard box.

"Glen. Come in. What are you doing here?"

Glen, taller of the two, offered the box to Seth. "I have a few more in the car." He went to get them and Seth stopped him.

"Later, I'll help you. Let me change first. Come on in."

Glen followed Seth into the kitchen and smiled when he spotted the camcorder.

"Lara's been talking about your production." He waved to the lens that quietly filmed on the counter. "I attended a lecture about children's thyroid disease at the Hilton on the island. Anna asked me to drop off the twin's baby clothes."

"Thanks, Glen. How's the family?" He actually liked Glen better than her other brother. He was a pediatrician, and lived in Rhode Island with his wife and four kids. Seth found himself always arrested by Glen's face. It was the male version of Lara, and while her porcelain skin looked lovely on her, it gave Glen an effeminate cast to his appearance. He was a bit too formal for Seth, but had a good heart. Seth tried not to curse around him.

"Kids are great. How's the job hunt?" Glen took the water that Seth offered him.

"It's tough. I went today and four hundred people showed up for the same job. I'm competing with kids just out of school, who are willing to work for less. I'm thinking of looking into a franchise."

"What kind?"

Seth was evasive. "I don't know. I'm afraid to risk what we have left on a sandwich shop.

Something's gotta come along. I've never not been able to find a job."

"Do you need money?" Glen asked softly. "No. Thanks." Seth felt his face heat up. They

were all so super educated, his wife's family. Each one was very successful at what they picked. He would die before he took a handout from them. He didn't want to be the loser husband. "We've been careful. We still have most of our wedding money and I really saved a lot last year before the firm closed."

"Your boss was despicable. It was terrible the way he closed the firm taking everyone's pension." "Yeah. Thank God I didn't invest there."

"Well, do you want to help me bring in the stuff? Where's Lara?"

"She had a check-up. Stay a bit. I know she's on the way home."

"What have you heard about the cicadas this summer?" Glen asked.

"Oh the usual. Come on, though. They come every year, so maybe there'll be a few more than usual. I'm not panicking. Your sister on the other hand..." Seth offered with a raised eyebrow.

Glen shrugged. "I know, but they are expecting something out of the ordinary. I'm sending the kids to my parents for the summer."

"Really? That's extreme."

"Well, I promised when they retired there, I would do it until they went to camp, so it's sort of an insurance policy. But, I do get a few weeks alone with Anna."

"Hmmm," Seth nodded. Anna was a Danish supermodel only one of Lara's brothers could have nailed. She was a Viking. Seth smirked and oddly enough, Glen smiled right back, each caught in the same thought.

Seth heard the garage door open and said, "Well you're in luck. Here she is."

He heard the garage door open and called out, "Lar, Lar. Your brother's here."

Lara squealed with delight and rushed into the room, quickly pecking Seth and then jumping into her brother's outstretched arms.

"You look adorable Lillypad!" Glen held her at arm's length. "I can't believe, our baby's having a baby."

Seth winced and wanted to tell her adoring brother she wasn't such a baby anymore.

"I gained three pounds this month." "That's not bad. You'll take it right off

afterwards," Glen responded. "Anna sent some boxes of baby clothes. She said to tell you, she scrubbed the stains out. They look brand new. Have you picked a name."

"We're still working on it. I like Spencer and Seth is stuck on Murray."

"Murray?"

"Yeah, Murray. It's different," Seth insisted.

Glen shrugged and replied, "Different is good."

Seth shot a triumphant look at Lara, once again in good charity with his brother-in-law.

"You're staying for dinner. I have enough," Lara announced as Glen started to protest.

Lara shushed him. "I won't hear of anything else."

*　*　*

Seth sighed gustily when he opened the door and saw a sea of UPS boxes piled on his front porch.

Everyday boxes started arriving, all from the registry and all a bunch of crap as far as he was concerned. Lara had filled three different registries in all the baby stores and now people were buying the gifts and sending it to them.

He brought in the latest batch and figured he better start opening them and getting rid of the boxes. Lara complained they bring bugs into the house.

There were bibs, onesies, bath toys, rubber ducks galore, changing pads, a nuclear diaper pail, skin care, rattles, baby Uggs, baby snot wipes. Seth shook his head as he unpacked all the junk.

The last box was immense and using a ballpoint pen, he slit it open. Reaching in, he lifted a stuffed pink unicorn on rockers. Dropping it back in the box, he yelled, "Lar…"

Looking at his in-laws return address on the box, he muttered, "Oh Murray… what were they thinking?"

"I'm up in the baby's room," Lara answered Seth shout. He took the steps two at a time.

"What's up buttercup?" he kissed the top of her head upon entering the nursery. She sat on the floor, surrounded by open boxes. In one corner were five different brands of diapers piled on top of each other. In a hamper were assorted teething rings and pacifiers. There must have been a hundred, Seth observed.

She had put together an infant seat and a play- mat that took up another whole corner of the room. Seth's football sat among the litter of stuffed animals.

"They got him a pink horse thing. With a horn in its head. It's not safe."

"It's a unicorn and it is safe. Boys can like unicorns too."

"Not Murray."

"We're moving on to Nathan. I like Nathan."

"It looks like a toy store exploded in here." "This is the tip of the iceberg. We need so much

more. I'm getting everything set up now. I want it done before I get too big. Do you like the walls?"

Seth looked at the vinyl transfers Lara had bought at the baby store that now adorned the light, blue walls.

"You bought bugs?" he asked disbelievingly. "I thought we were doing a safari theme."

"That's all they had in the stores. Aren't they cute. Look at the trail of ants going up the tree." She pointed to an army of cute cartoonish insects climbing up the walls to a beehive hanging from the illustration of a tree.

"It's creepy Lar. I don't like it."

"Well, I do!" she pouted and that was the end of that.

* * *

"Man, I'm getting hungry." Seth rubbed his belly. Admiring his body in the bedroom mirror, he looked at himself sideways. "Too much pickles and ice cream," he thought. He was wearing a bathing suit and holding the pervasive camcorder in his hand.

"Seth," a very pregnant Lara called. "Put the chicken on the grill. They're here."

Seth raised one eyebrow in the mirror and repeated, "They're here?" in a chilling voice.

He peeked downstairs. Lara was hugging her best friend in the hallway. "I hope you brought your suits. It turned out to be sunny," he overheard.

"You don't even look pregnant. Dominic, isn't she the cutest thing?"

Seth slowly descended the stairs thinking this was only going to be an hour. He kept repeating that mantra in his head hoping it would make him feel better.

Marni Halverston was rubbing Lara's belly, and while Seth had on a phony smile, deep down inside he was totally grossed out.

Any other guy on this planet would be too shy to ask Marni for her number. She was a hot tamale.

Curly sandy-blonde hair cascaded down her narrow back. She had deep brown eyes with luscious lashes and a mischievous dimple on either side of her pouting lips. Spending hours at the gym, she sweated out any fat that could be taking up a centimeter on her body. Her figure alone turned heads wherever they went. She was every boy's crush in school. Hell, she was every guy's crush, no matter where she went.

Seth could have had the opportunity to sleep with her in college, but he met Lara at the mixer first. It crossed his mind briefly when they met, but he was more attracted to Lara's personality. Marni was good for a couple nights. Lara would be good for the rest of his life. It was an easy decision, and he never regretted it.

Lara was blushing and talking to her friend in a high-pitched, super sweet voice. She was sounding more and more like Kim Kardashian by the second. Hating this fake side of Lara, he caught her eye and gagged.

Every single time she saw Marni, this overwhelming giddiness came over Lara. It made Seth sick. He dealt with it in college. Even after college for the dozen times he'd had to see Marni, he let his wife act all stupid in front of her. Marni was a troublemaker. She constantly stirred the pot, creating issues and drama. He knew she had spread a vicious rumor about him cheating. He never did and Lara would never forgive her for it.

"What's with the camera, Seth?" asked Marni.

Seth paused and was about to say something rude and condescending, but he caught Lara's silly grin. If Lara didn't have ears, the tips of her lips would be touching. She was so incredibly happy to see her friend that Seth felt it would be just plain evil to destroy it. So, if his wife wanted to get all nostalgic on him, who was he to burst her bubble. Seth might be Lara's numero uno, but Marni came in a very, very close second. It was too cruel to hurt her.

Instead of sounding like a jerk, he spoke confidently, "I'm filming a documentary."

"About what?"

"Friends with herp…" Much as he tried, he couldn't help himself as he watched Marni's condescending smirk.

"He's filming my pregnancy!" interjected Lara. "That's so cute! Thanks for inviting us, Sethy."

Marni gave him the phony double-cheek kiss.

"What? Are we in Europe?" he asked as she retreated and disappeared into the kitchen with his wife.

Dominic sheepishly looked at him with dark- brown eyes and shrugged. "It's all from that. They all think they're tray cheek."

"Tray Cheek?" replied Seth.

"You know. French."

"Oh," The light bulb went off for Seth. "Tres chic."

"Not chic, cheek."

Seth wasn't going to waste another second on semantics with Dominic. Even if he wanted to, Dominic would have been too busy studying his pecks in the entry hall mirror. Stupid tribal tattoos covered both his arms. He used every opportunity to show off his six-pack. Seth could never understand why Dominic needed all that ink. What was he going to do when the six-pack sagged and turned into a beer barrel? Both of Dom's parents were overweight.

Dominic was ripped. Working out was like a second job for him. He was a gym rat. Last Seth heard, he got a great job in sales somewhere. Must be a gym, Seth shrugged.

"Wanna beer?" asked Seth.

"You buying?" Dominic asked, looking at his slicked-back hair in the mirror.

"Well, we know you're not!" Seth thought but then replied, "It's good to have you as our guest, Dom."

The guys left for the kitchen in search of alcohol. As they entered the kitchen, the room got quiet and Seth knew the girls were having a serious conversation. About what he could only guess. Lara looked worried.

Marni motioned Dom to leave the room with her and nodded to Lara.

Both Marni and Dominic made a quick exit. Seth was dumbfounded.

"That was quick. Was it something I said?" "Well…" Lara busied herself with chopping vegetables at the sink. "Well…"

"What's going on, Lara?" Seth felt a cold chill go up his spine. When Lara started any sentence with "well," there was always a rub. Something smelled weird. Lara knew something, and she wasn't telling her husband.

"Well what, Lara? Spit it out."

"They were evicted." Lara turned to him, her cleaver in midair.

"You gonna use that?" He pointed to the knife. "Oh." She quickly put it down on the cutting board. "I felt so bad. She would do anything for us, you know."

"That's rather easy because we never ask." "There for the grace of God go I," Lara

righteously stated. "You're still looking for a job. What if you don't get it, Seth? We've been lucky because we had some savings, but what if… ?" She paused. "I know she would do anything for us."

Seth started to feel bad for Marni and for Lara, even though he felt he shouldn't. He knew Lara wasn't joking. Seth wasn't working, and he had an acquaintance he had known for over a decade who was homeless. Lara's soulful looks tugged at his heart. Much as he didn't want to admit it, he knew they would have to do the right thing.

The economy sucked. The government promised

more—more help, more jobs, more growth. Seth and everyone he knew wanted that change that never came. Here were people in the same boat.

"Have I ever let you down? No, don't answer that. I'll get a job, Lara. You'll never have to ask Marni for help."

He looked deep into her distressed face. "You are such a bleeding heart," Seth said sympathetically. "OK, you can keep them, but you have to take care of them. Make sure they don't pee on the rug."

* * *

"Get the orange juice." Dom said as he prepared a cup for the coffee maker. He spun the rack, "Don't they have anything but decaf."

"Ugh. I know." Marni made a face. "It's like low carb this, low fat that. She is the worst cook in the world."

"That's your friend. Is there any bread?' "Whole wheat muffins?" Marni took a bite.

"They're like sawdust." She rooted around the pantry. "Kashi, kashi and more kashi. Do you want to go out?'

"With what money?" Dominic opened the refrigerator. "Look, cream cheese, a soy variety.

What is Seth eating?" he continued to poke around the fridge. "Pay dirt!"

"What? What did you find?"

"Salami. It's wrapped in a brown bag. You can't hide good food from Dominic DiLeo. I am a hunter!" he roared.

"Yeah, but what can I eat? I don't like tubed meat." Marni stared at the open fridge.

"Since when?" Dom was stuffing his face with the salami. "See if there's any cheese."

Marni took out a container of cottage cheese and ate right out of the plastic cup. "I saw some chips and dip in the laundry room pantry."

Dom unfolded himself from the chair. "Let me appropriate it and bring it upstairs before they come home."

She heard him digging through a closet in the laundry room.

"Oh, you won't believe this, there's packets of water," he shouted back.

"What?" Marni asked, her mouth full of swiss cheese.

"Water. If we take this, we don't have to bring up the bottles in front of them. I swear Seth's been giving me dirty looks every time I take a bottle of the water."

"Take the whole box, they won't miss it."

She heard Dom race up the stairs. Bending low, she found a bag of chocolate kisses. "Holding out on me, huh, Lara. I knew you had a secret stash somewhere." Marni raced up the stairs after Dom, her hands filled with Lara's candy treasure.

*   *   *

They all sat at the kitchen table, cards strewn about, half-filled glasses and bowls of snack food.

"Another game?" Dominic reeled in a pile of quarters.

"I'm pooped." Seth stretched.

Marni eyed Dominic's growing pile of coins and urged, "One more game. Come on, you guys."

Lara stood up and started moving things to the sink. She yawned loudly. "I don't know about you, but I'm tired."

"Leave it, babe. I'll clean it up," Seth volunteered.

"I gotta piss. Marni grab the change and bring it upstairs." Dominic beat a hasty retreat to the guest bedroom.

Marni scooped the winnings into a cup and followed him, Seth watched with wide-eyed fascination at their gall.

"I don't believe them." He put his glass forcefully on the granite counter. "They eat like they each have two assholes. Do you know they ate up that Spanish ham your brother sent me? Just took it and finished it, without even asking." He paused. "I want to know what happened with playing with bobby pins or peanuts."

"Yeah." Lara averted her eyes, "that was pretty crummy for them to insist we play for real money. We didn't lose much, Seth. It's just pocket change."

"That's not the point!" He washed out the coffee cups. "This is too much. I don't like them, Lara. It's enough. They're taking advantage of us. It's time for them to go home."

Lara sighed and put her china away.

CHAPTER 6
EMERGE

"Change doth unknit the tranquil strength of men."

- Matthew Arnold

THEIR BACKYARD WAS expansive, just as wide as the front. A suburban heaven, they had lavished a ton of their wedding money on the yard.

Dominic was chipping on a mini backyard putting green off to the left, while the girls sunned themselves in skimpy bikinis on chaise lounges.

Seth had a smoker, a gas grill, a charcoal grill, and fire pit. He never used any of them but the gas grill because it was the easiest to clean. When he was working, he bought every toy he could for his backyard, especially the grilling station.

At the far back was an in-ground pool surrounded by a deep black fence. Seth manned the gas grill.

"I'm putting up the sausages." Seth dropped the camera on the custom-made picnic table.

"I thought we were having chicken," Lara piped up.

"You," said Seth, pointing his tongs at her, "thought wrong." He left for the kitchen.

Marni peeked over her shoulder and in a whisper asked Lara, "Is he at least trying to get a job?"

Lara knew it was coming. She looked back to ensure Seth was deep in the kitchen.

"He said hiring is slow this summer. A lot of people have left, and with the infestation, it's like they are afraid to spend or create jobs."

"Oh, come on, Lara. Anyone can get him a job tomorrow."

"Shh," Lara warned, "he'll hear you." Sniffing, a little miffed, she wanted to ask her friend why she was complaining about Seth when she was the one who lost her apartment, but good manners demanded the subject be dropped.

The screen slid open and Seth picked up the camera again.

"Are you going to heat up the pool?" Lara asked politely with her voice high and nervous.

Seth walked down the hill to the pool with camera in hand. The grass was slightly overgrown and needed a mowing. They had let the gardener go last week; it was getting a little too expensive. Seth thought maybe he would have Jimmy come by and do a quick trim.

As he reached the pool filter, he flipped the switch on. Pressing the motor, the filter came alive with the comforting sounds of a pool backwash.

He moved over to the big-box heater unit. Bending

down, he reached through a tangle of weeds, freezing, his hand came in contact with a slippery shell.

"What the…?" He peered around the unit. There it was, in living color. The brown cicada shell was about the size of Seth's pinky. He had never seen an exoskeleton that big before.

It was wet, with a crusty brown shell exterior. It was split down the middle, and he knew that somewhere in his yard was a bug the size of a clothes pin.

"Wow." Seth was awed. "What are we going to do now? Call nine-one-one? Alert the military? How about we get CNN down here to discuss the mating habits of these fine creatures?"

Seth peeled the shell off the heater unit and examined it. Sniffing it, he backed away from the crypt like, musty smell.

Dropping it to the ground, he crushed it with the sole of his flip-flop.

"It's gonna be a turkey shoot, heh-heh," he snickered.

Looking back, he saw Lara at the deck, her hand shading her eyes as she scanned the yard looking for Seth. Thank goodness she didn't have great eyesight. The questions would be nonstop for the rest of the summer. "What was it? Was it gross? Did it bite? Was it scary? Did you touch it?"

Seth wasn't in the mood for hysterics or an interrogation. He said the only thing he could think of to get everyone ready for the next activity as he played host,

"Pool's open!"

* * *

The foursome floated in the refreshing water as the camera filmed them from the pool coping.

Sunlight danced on the dappled surface. Lara's nose was tinged pink. Seth fought the urge to kiss its upturned tip. She had been so moody lately.

The reality of pregnancy was in full drive. Lara felt gross. Cumbersome as a beached whale, she was getting fatter as the days went by. At night she got round ligament pains and it drove her to tears. Her tight belly stretched to accommodate his growing child.

He dove underwater and swam up behind her. Pulling her into his arms, he kissed the top of her head. They silently floated lazily in the shallow end.

"Oh, that's so cute," Marni trilled.

Seth thought her voice was like nails to a chalkboard.

"How come you never do that to me, Dom?" Marni complained.

"You're not pregnant." He dove quickly and resurfaced, his black hair slick against his skull.

Lara was floating on Seth's chest and stomach. Her belly and face were the only body parts above the surface of the water.

Seth was gazing in the distance. He noticed something on a tree and froze. As he stopped the motion to continue floating, Lara sank a bit getting chlorinated water in the corners of her mouth.

He could have sworn it was a tiny bird, or even a chipmunk, but the thing actually glided down from a tree. It couldn't be an insect. Coming up sputtering, she glared at him.

"Don't tease me like that. It's bad enough I'm swimming in all these chemicals, now you want me to drink the water." She noticed Seth wasn't paying her any attention.

"What's wrong?" continued Lara. "You look like you've seen a ghost." Lara turned in the direction Seth was looking to see what got his attention.

Seth shook his head. "Nothing. I thought I saw something."

Lara turned back to him. "Seth, I know that look. What did you see?"

He changed the subject. "Water's nice, right?"

"Yeah," Lara replied dubiously. "It's perfect."

They waded in silence as Seth thought about what he just witnessed. The broken shell really didn't faze him until he saw the actual insect scurry down a tree. It was like staring at a familiar place and seeing a gnome run across the yard with an ice pick. It gained your attention. It certainly got Seth's attention. Seth floated lost in thought, his eyes searching suspiciously everywhere.

"How about some drinks?" Lara said as she attempted to break the suddenly sour mood.

"What a great idea." Seth gave Lara a look that didn't bode well. It was bad enough that he was extending his accommodations to people he couldn't stand, but this was too much. Seth had recently reviewed their expenses, and spending on Marni and Dominic's wine requirements wasn't in the budget.

"Yeah, our treat," Dominic offered.

Seth knew it was more of Dominic's bullshit. The guy never went to his pocket for anything. It was tiresome. They would get to the bar, drink to their hearts content and Dominic would somehow find himself in the bathroom when the check came.

Marni was conveniently oblivious.

The truth was they were all bored. Enough sun, enough talk, and enough company.

To Seth, it was like contacting a friend you knew really well in college. He got that nostalgic feeling and talked about the good old days for a little too long. Then the conversation dried up and it was time to move on. You sat and wondered why it was so important to reconnect with that person. Having nothing in common, you had to admit that some things should remain in the past. Jimmy's words echoed in his brain. "Gone. Kaput. Finished." Seth groaned.

Summer should be over already. He wanted to be able to kick them out politely so he and his wife could enjoy the company of their new family—just the three of them. No stragglers. But summer was just about to get started. They had a few months before things really changed.

* * *

The phone was ringing off the hook. Lara called from the bedroom where she was changing. "Are you going to get that?" Seth looked at the caller ID and winced. "Seth!"

Picking up the receiver, he cleared his throat. "Hi,

Ruth. Fine. No we're fine. I don't know why she hasn't, uh…No, I'm still looking. Hold on a minute."

He covered the receiver and called his wife. "Lara, it's your mom. Come here and talk to her or I'm gonna hang up."

Seth got back on the phone. "Oh, hi, Artie. It's just a bunch of nonsense. No, no, we don't want to come to Arizona right now. She's fine; we're fine. It's all hype. Really, Artie, I'm more afraid of the rattlesnakes in Arizona than cicadas in the Northeast. Oh, here's Lara now." He handed her the phone with a look of warning.

"Hi, Daddy. You are so sweet. Seth's got it all covered. He bought extra water, we have canned…of course I got the safe ones, no lead, right.

I know…" She was nodding her head in assent. "He just pretends to be a wise guy; he really takes good care of me…No, don't do that. We are perfectly fine. Yes, yes… yes. Uh-huh, yes. I will. We were just on our way out. Yes, yes, OK. I will." There was a long pause, her eyes welling up. "I always listen to you."

She looked with a pleading expression to Seth, who was now punching in a number on his cell.

"Oh, Dad, there's a beep. I'm getting another call. It could be the doctor. No, nothing is wrong. Yes, I'll tell Dr. Roman you said hi. I'll call you Wednesday. Yesss. Wednesday, right…there it is again. Love you. Kisses."

"No, no, no," said Seth. "Please tell me they are not coming."

"Good thinking with the phone," replied Lara. "Nope. They are so cute. They're just worried about the infestation."

"If they come, it's a worst infestation," Seth grumbled. He heard Marni and Dom heading out the door. "I don't know what's worse, leeches," he said and nodded to Marni, "or killer bees." he pointed to his in-laws' pictures.

"Oh, please. Old friends, concerned family…it's all good." Lara chuckled good-naturedly.

*　*　*

Piling into Lara's car, they pulled out of the subdivision. Marni was scoping out the power windows like a child. She was also playing with Seth's camera, filming everything from the backseat.

"An SUV! Ooh la la," Marni exclaimed. "Mercedes, no less. How'd you manage that?"

There was always an underlying jealousy between Marni and Lara. No matter how much Marni loved Lara, sometimes the green-eyed monster appeared.

She was resentful that Lara lived in a beautiful house on the North Shore of Long Island. To be fair, Lara admitted she was a bit jealous of Marni's five-foot-nine frame and supermodel figure. There wasn't resentment, just a touch of envy.

Lara never liked to brag about her lifestyle because Marni made her feel guilty. She certainly would have never told her over the phone about the Mercedes being a present from her parents.

"Gee, the town's deserted," Dominic noted, sitting in the front with Seth. Except for their car driving through the town, the streets were empty. It was odd, the sound of silence. Not even planes were flying overhead. No birds chirping, no car doors slamming. "It is deserted," Seth thought.

"And with a sunroof, wow!" Marni continued. "Please," Marni pleaded with Seth, "can we open it?"

Seth smiled, all his teeth in a creepy grin, and opened the sunroof.

He eyed his wife in the backseat, realizing she had had enough and getting some pleasure knowing that tonight she was going to hear "Serves you right." Company was fine for a couple hours, but this was getting ridiculous. What did Benjamin Franklin say about fish and visitors, something about them both stinking within three days? That would make some useful repartee tonight, he thought wickedly.

"Yes, the car was a gift from my parents. They give us one super-duper gift a year. Right, Seth?"

"Super-duper," Seth agreed sarcastically. Lara met his eyes in the mirror with a sweet smile.

That stung Marni a bit. All she ever got from her parents was criticism. With Marni's third-grade salary, it was impossible to make ends meet, Dominic's DJ jobs brought little home, and his sales job was another story altogether.

"You're so lucky," Marni replied. "Mine forget they even have a daughter."

"I said..." Dominic interrupted, apparently not finished with his subject. "The town is empty. You think it's that cicada thing everyone's talking about?"

"Oh, cicadas are so last year," said Seth. "I hear zombies are invading this month."

As Seth finished the word , in what seemed like slow motion, a three-inch cicada came falling through the sunroof and landed belly up on the armrest.

Dominic was the first to react and tried to get as close to the passenger-side window without falling out of it. Seth lost control of the car. It could have been from the bug or the other three screaming their heads off.

"Get it outta here!" Dominic yelled.

Seth fought to gain control of the car. The bug was rolling on its back with the jerky movement with the car. It finally rolled over to its feet and noticed the commotion. Buzzing furiously, it took off trying to escape. It hit Seth in his face as it tried to get past him to the open window, but Seth, in a quick reflex, swatted the bug back into the car.

Desperately, it flew into the back. The girls' screams echoed through the interior. Now the bug flew back to the front and landed on Dominic's chest.

"Get it off!" Dominic's back was pushed up against the seat as Seth tried to pull over.

The louder the girls yelled, the faster the cicada fluttered its wings. Its hard, spiny legs clung to Dominic's shirt, irritating his chest. The legs easily tore through the cotton T-shirt he was wearing.

Dominic felt the spiny legs latch onto his chest, freaking him out even more.

"Where is the ice scraper?" Seth yelled.

Lara grabbed an umbrella from the backseat and tried smacking it but only succeeded in jabbing Seth.

"Lara, quit it! You're just pissing it and me off more!"

Seth snatched the umbrella from her in a vicious tug, and he and Dominic were able to throw the invader out the window.

They all quickly closed their windows.

"What was that thing!?" exclaimed Marni. "It was a cicada." Seth was out of breath.

Dominic's face was planted in his hands. He was swaying back and forth.

"Whoa, that was big! It was prehistoric," Dominic muttered from behind his hands.

"They're fat, lazy, and harmless," said Seth. "How long did it take to kill it? Two seconds? They are scaring the public with all this crazy talk."

"That was disgusting," Lara shuddered.

"But that bug was slow and cumbersome. Even you could take it, Lara. And you're a hundred pounds dripping wet."

Always honest, Lara replied, "Really a hundred and twenty-eight."

"Oh, a real heavyweight. I told you there was nothing to worry about. Did it bite you, Dom?" Seth turned to Dominic.

"But the size of that thing," said Marni. Didn't even faze old Dom here, did it?"

Not wanting to appear any less macho, Dominic agreed. "It was like shooting ducks in a barrel."

"You mean fish?"

"What? No ducks," Dominic repeated. "It was really no big deal. Once you get over the size, they're really easy to kill. It did try to pierce me with a stinger. It looked like it wanted to poke holes in my body."

"That's because you're so good looking. What's another piercing with all your other body jewels?" Seth tried to lighten the mood in the car. "It looked just like the one I saw by the pool."

Seth knew their reaction was going to go two ways. Either they were going to laugh at the comment, knowing Seth was just messing around, or they were going to freak out.

"What!?" exclaimed Lara.

Seth thought it was too late to pull out of the dive.

"Thanks for telling us," Marni spat.

"There was one in the pool?" Dominic was dumbfounded. "I didn't see any cicada in your pool."

"Yeah, it was doing the backstroke," Seth quipped. "You didn't see it?"

No one knew what the hell Seth was talking about. He could turn the sentence into a joke or tell them the truth. This was why nobody liked him.

Always testing, he liked to see what he could get away with without really answering.

"In all seriousness, it was by a tree. It was big but seemed harmless," Seth said.

"Was it dead?" Lara asked in a small voice. She locked eyes with Seth in the mirror. "Do you think it's starting?" she added, her eyes wide with panic.

Seth started humming the music from. "It was nothing. They're too big to run."

"Why didn't you say anything?" Lara asked softly.

"Because it was no big deal," Seth answered and reassured her with a saucy wink.

"Enough cicada talk." Marni wanted to change to subject.

"Now you're speaking my language, Marni," said Seth. By now they had all calmed down. The conversation moved on.

"Have you picked a name yet?" Marni asked. "Marshall," Seth said at the same time as Lara said, "Mason."

"Is that all you got?" Marni laughed, all tension gone. "You guys are a riot."

"Yeah, like a barrel of cicadas." Seth pulled into the bar.

* * *

Lara was on one knee trying to dig out a pot to use for dinner.

"Let me help," Seth offered her a hand. "Why are you doing this alone? Where's the devil's handmaiden?"

"Stop, Marni offered to help. It's easier to do it by myself." She walked over to the pantry. "Humph."

"What'sa matter, hon?"

"Oh nothing. I thought I bought enough food, but I guess we used it up."

"Four is a lot to feed, Lar. Have you thought about cutting our guests loose. More toilet paper, paper towels, laundry detergent. Cheese, milk, eggs, salami… I will keep going if you don't stop me."

"Stop. I don't mind. It's only supplies. I'll go shopping tomorrow."

"Send them. It's the least they can do," Seth snapped. "Do you know where my pork rinds are?"

"I don't want you to eat those." Lara called out to him

as he rummaged the pantry. "Try the laundry room. I kept some extra stuff there."

"Out, out and out. I think the infestation has started."

Lara dropped the pan she was holding. "What, Seth. You mean cicadas?" she said nervously.

"No, rats. Two big legged rats." Seth slammed out of the house.

*   *   *

The next day, Lara gazed out her big picture window, clearly annoyed. "I thought you spoke to Jeff and Cathy about that dog."

"I did. What's he up to now?" Seth asked. "Well, hello, little lady." He raised the ubiquitous camera as a basset hound strolled into the yard. "Looks like Casey is gonna get some nookie."

"Go out and stop them. Ugh. Not on my watch. Jeez, look at him!"

They both laughed as the bigger, sandy-colored lab mounted a basset hound.

"Well, someone's not going to be too happy with that," said Seth, nodding to the humping dogs.

"Do you know who owns the basset?" Lara giggled.

The sliding door was open, a breeze wafting into the house.

"Do you hear that?" Lara turned to Seth. "What?"

"That's it. It went completely silent outside," Lara whispered.

"Probably a hawk is circling. Maybe they're watching the porn… What the hell?"

A deafening yelp erupted from Casey, and he started biting his left rear leg. The basset threw herself on the ground and rolled, howling as if she had been dowsed with acid.

"Seth," Lara screamed, as a blanket of black bugs descended on the tormented animals, obliterating them from sight. The roar of cicadas filled the front yard, and Seth opened the door to go and help the dogs.

"Noooo," Lara gripped his arm. "You can't."

"I have to, Lara. This is crazy. Call animal control."

Grabbing a broom, he raced over the green grass to the now still hill of insects.

Grimly he swept off the unresisting cicadas from the corpses of the dogs.

"Shit," was all he could say.

*　*　*

The wail of sirens rent the air, and Seth burst through the front door holding the camera to see what was happening.

Lara followed him out with a dishrag clenched in her hands.

"What's going on now?" she asked nervously.

"I don't know," Seth responded. "I heard a crash. It was loud. Look, there it is," he pointed to the end of the block. "Stay inside."

Lara retreated into the house.

A crowd of people had gathered around two cars that had hit each other head on. The black BMW was badly banged up. The chassis was nearly bent in half and steam rose from its hood. The air bag deployed and filled the entire front of the car. The door was open and a man was sitting in the driver's seat, talking on his cell phone.

A silver Prius rested atop a broken fire hydrant. A geyser of water roared as it shot ten feet into the air.

Sitting on the curb, a dazed woman was holding a towel to her bloody nose. His neighbor Cathy dashed out of her house to comfort the woman.

"Are you OK?" Seth wandered over to the stricken woman.

"I don't know what happened," the woman replied. "I was driving and out of nowhere the whole windshield was covered by bugs."

"Cicadas?" Seth inquired.

"I don't know what they were. But there were a lot of them. The wipers couldn't get rid of them quick enough. They just kept coming."

Seth walked away as the woman started to cry.

He looked at the totaled car. A brown residue of bug guts smeared the windshield.

Police cars started rolling down the street and pretty soon the chaotic mess got sorted out.

A cop walked over to survey the scene next to Seth. He turned to the policeman and asked, "What do you make of this?"

The officer shrugged his shoulders and replied, "Probably just a swarm."

* * *

Later that night, Lara curled against Seth's side, they watched the evening news.

The newscaster was concluding a segment, "There are widespread and unprovoked bug attacks all over the tri-state area today causing accidents and mayhem everywhere. Although it was very disturbing, the governor is assuring everyone to remain calm. Cicadas usually die within a day or two. He is urging people not to panic."

"I feel so bad for Cathy," Lara's blue eyes welled with tears. "She loved that dog. This is getting scary, Seth."

"You heard what the cops said. They probably disturbed a nest. That's what happened in Arizona too you know, with the killer bees. They have people there who just take out the nests for a living."

"What about the car accident?" Lara asked. Seth put a finger over her soft lips.

"They told us not to be concerned. The cops were here in four minutes, and animal control said not to blow it out of proportion. Enough!" He kissed her lightly. "I said enough."

* * *

"I stocked up. Don't you remember Lara. It was after we bought that stupid freezer. I bought two of everything. I spent close to eight hundred dollars." Seth was furious. "What do you mean we are out of tuna? I bought rice, beans, all kinds of canned shit. We can't be out."

"We are for now. I guess I didn't realize how much we were going through. I'm sorry Seth."

"Ah ha. I knew it. They are eating us out of house and home," Seth was angry. "They gotta go."

"Just another week," Lara pleaded. "I promise I will speak to Marni."

"Freeloaders. I never saw anything like this. I thought my mom was bad. They take it to a whole new level. That's it. I want them outta here." Seth went outside to shoot some hoops, the screen door slammed behind him.

* * *

"Let's go for sushi tonight," Marni said gaily. "Lara can't eat that, "Seth replied morosely. "Chinese?" Dom volunteered.

"Nope," Seth walked over to the counter and started making a cheese sandwich.

"Come on Seth, let's go somewhere." Marni started to put on her jacket.

"See ya later. Lara, you want one too?" He held up a slice of bread.

Clearly torn, her face a mask of appeasement, she walked over to Seth and stroked his back. "You feel like a steak?" she asked hopefully.

"You don't want to know what I feel like," he continued with his sandwich.

"I can't believe it Seth. It's dinner time. What do you expect us to do?" Marni shrieked at him.

"I don't care what you do, Marn. I am eating here, now. I am not going out. I am tired of paying the bill."

"Maybe I was going to pay for tonight!" Marni shouted.

"He's got you there, babe," Dom came over to the counter. "You got any more cheese?"

Seth nodded to the refrigerator, gave Marni a dirty look and with an expression that boded ill for tonight, he went into the den to watch the rest of a game.

* * *

The camera was charging on the counter while news from a television droned in the kitchen.

Reports of encounters with the cicadas were all over the news.

"It kept batting into our Florida room," the man on the television said. "Finally, I took a broom and whacked it."

"Seen any others?" the reporter asked.

"Here and there, but I think we've got it under control. Aside from the noise, which is annoying, we seem to be able…"

Marni slid onto a counter stool next to Lara with her coffee, muttering, "He was such an asshole the other night."

"I didn't notice. I thought Dominic behaved."

Marni gave her a long look from beneath her ginger-colored lashes. "I was talking about Seth."

"Look, Marn. He's a good guy. He takes care of me." Marni snorted inelegantly as Lara continued, "He makes me laugh."

"Yeah. He makes me laugh too, but not in the same way. I can't believe he's been out of work this long."

"Marn, what happened with your apartment?"

Marni bristled. "I thought I could tell you anything; apparently since you're having his baby things have changed."

"What are you talking about?" Lara hissed.

Seth entered the kitchen. He gave a stunning smile to his wife, then a grimace to her friend, "Good morning, Marni."

Marni stood and smirked back at Seth. "I'll let you two enjoy some private time. God knows how much longer you'll have for that." She stalked off to find Dominic.

"Dom?" she called to no answer. He finally appeared in the kitchen doorway, fresh out of the shower.

"Hoops?" Dominic asked Seth.

"You girls rustle up some breakfast while we go practice our jumping skills. We're getting ready for the infestation!"

"Get your own breakfast, Seth," Marni sneered. "I heard it on the news this morning. We have to practice jumping per the National Cicada Prevention Society. Watch."

He leaped into the air, "Jump and squash. Right, Dom? Jump and squash. I have to do Lara's share, as she's confined to skipping until Rudolph arrives."

Dominic laughed and threw a basketball to Seth, who deftly caught it. "I have to remember that jump and squash."

"Take the camcorder so we can show your kid how I kicked your ass," Dom added.

"It's charging. Let's go."

Marni and Lara exchanged looks and started taking out things from the refrigerator.

"OK, they're both assholes," Marni conceded as she and Lara watched their retreating backs.

Years ago Seth had set up a regulation basketball hoop

on the patio just off the deck in their backyard. He had been the high school point guard and always had a fondness for the game. Dominic would play, but he was terrible. He wanted to look good first and play good second.

Seth had more control with the ball. He was accomplished enough to play well and look good at the same time. He gave it up during college because he gained too much weight from drinking. Once he found his perfect home with Lara, the flat screen and the basketball hoop were the first purchases he made.

It never bothered Lara that he liked to play so much. It gave her some time to straighten up the house while he shot hoops alone. If the weather was sunny and over forty degrees, he would be outside. He would take hoops solo over jogging with his wife any day of the week.

The girls heard the ball bouncing off the rim through the screen door in the kitchen.

Marni was standing by the door, drying a pan and watching their play.

"I don't mean to harp," Marni said in reverie. "I sometimes think I'm displacing my own anger."

Lara was hoping to get an apology from her for calling Seth an asshole. She was fighting with Seth over Marni staying and questioning herself if her friend was really worth the struggle with Seth.

"Dom lost his job last Tuesday."

Lara felt her pain. She was going through the same thing and knew how hard it was. Her sense of resentment completely evaporated.

"What?" Lara stopped whipping eggs to look up at her friend.

"His sales dropped. That's why we lost the apartment. I couldn't keep up with the payments. My salary's been frozen for three years. No raises. I got a part-time job just to help, but it started affecting our relationship. He said I emasculated him. He could support us. If not for all this cicada crap, people would be spending more."

"Seth says the same thing. I don't know what to tell my parents anymore." Lara moved closer. "He's been even asking at the gas station if he could pump gas," she sighed. "I felt like he was finally growing up. You know, no job was beneath him.

Maybe this whole thing is a good thing in some small way."

They heard a shout followed by a scream. "What?" Marni yelled, dropping the pan. "What

was that? Dom, Dom, are you OK?"

She opened the screen door to a panicked Seth. "Close the door and stay inside!" He pointed at Marni without taking his eyes off Dominic.

"What's the matter?" Lara put down the eggs and walked over to the door.

"I saw something fly into Dom's chest," Marni screamed. "I don't see him now. Look, I'm coming out!" Lara grabbed the camcorder without listening and followed Marni.

"Help!" Dom was on the brick patio with Seth circling him, completely flustered. "Get them off." Dom was breathless. "Ow, ow, ow," he started moaning.

"Damn it!" Seth screamed. "Move your arms, Dom. I have to grab them!"

On top of Dominic was a cluster of cicada. They covered his groin next to his pubic bone. Shaking furiously they fluttered their wings violently.

The girls started crying.

"Dom!" Marni cringed. "Seth, get it off him!" "I can't! His arms are in the way."

Seth started yanking the cicadas off his body. He felt one of the bug's abdomen tense. The threatened cicada let out a shrill that drowned out the girls' screaming.

Dominic wailed. Everyone watched helplessly as the cicada jolted down his abdomen, stabbing Dominic in the stomach with its stinger. Snot was shooting from Dominic's nose, his face bright red.

There was nothing they could do. Seth tried kicking it, but it clung tighter to Dom's shirt. Blood starting pouring out of the incision the bug just made. The insect's legs planted themselves in his skin.

"Oh my God!" Marni screamed and rushed to help Seth.

"Get into the house, Lara," Seth shouted over his shoulder.

"I'm calling the police." Lara handed the camcorder to Marni and ran for the phone.

"Call an ambulance!" said Marni in hysterics. Seth slowly pried the bug off of his friend. He grabbed the basketball and smashed it, goo squirting up at both Marni and him.

He removed his shirt and kneeled down to press it on a wheezing Dominic. Applying pressure, he tried to stop the bleeding. He surveyed the little cuts the bug made with their legs, but the gash that it left in Dominic's belly was what was most worrisome.

"We have to get him to a hospital," Marni said frantically.

Seth helped Dominic stand and put his arm under Dom's shoulder. He half-carried him into the house. Meanwhile, the wail of sirens in the distance gave them comfort. Seth thought, "Wow, that's Oyster Bay. Lara picked up the phone, and the cops are on their way."

Something didn't seem right. Lara went into the house just a few minutes ago, and now there are ambulances screeching down the block.

He didn't want to make anyone even more frightened, so he said the only positive thing he could think of. "Oh good, the ambulance is here."

Lara came out with the portable phone. "Nine-one-one never answered. What's going on?"

Dominic was turning paler than parchment as the seconds passed. "It hurts so much."

"Keep my shirt on there, buddy," Seth warned. "Get me another shirt, Lara."

Lara was standing, frozen, staring at the reddening cloth on Dominic's stomach. Marni was getting the keys. "Lara!" Seth barked, "help Marni find the keys and get my license and another shirt."

Lara jerked into action, but Marni came out with a bag, another towel, and the keys in her mouth.

"Don't worry, honey. We're taking you to the hospital.

They'll sew it up, one, two, three. Lara, move! We don't have time," Marni urged.

They moved their way through the kitchen and through the garage entrance. Seth helped Dominic get into the SUV. Both girls climbed into the backseat, Lara slower than Marni.

With the garage door open, they noticed several ambulances speeding up and down their street, sirens blaring as they came and went. Seth jumped in the driver's side. Slamming the SUV into reverse, he sped out.

CHAPTER 7
INFEST

"And they shall cover the face of the earth, that one cannot be able to see the earth…"

- Exodus 10:5

"DON'T YOU HAVE another emergency room in this hick town?" Marni screamed at Seth.

"I'll go in and stay with them," Lara said to Seth.

They were parked in the packed hospital parking lot.

"No. I don't think so," he gave Marni a dirty look. "I don't want you going in there," he said to Lara. "You don't know if people are sick or what. I don't want you catching anything." He exited the car. "Stay here, I'll be right out. I just want to know what's going on."

"At least document it for me with the camera, soI'll

know too," Lara said concerned. "Keep the sunroof closed," he ordered.

Inside, the corridors were packed with dazed patients. Many were holding towels or rags to seemingly minor bites or cuts like Dominic. Most were children, their parents hovering over them. Here and there you could see someone cradling a broken limb, probably a victim of an accident that resulted in avoiding bug attacks. All in all, it was not a bloodbath, but there were a lot of alarmed people.

Seth found Marni and Dom on the floor in the corridor that lead into the elevator for employees.

"Why are you here? They'll never call you." "They put us here," Marni spat.

"Hey, Marni, it's not my fault."

"You chose to live in this shithole called..." "Hey, I didn't ask you to stay."

"Kids, kids," Dom laughed weakly. "Can we save the argument for later? I'm hurting here."

"Sorry," Seth nodded. Marni bowed her head, tears welling in her cocoa eyes.

"Really, it's nothing. Just don't fight. Seth, we're gonna be here for a couple of hours. Take Lara home and we'll call you when to pick us up."

"You sure?"

"Yeah, no sense in all of us wasting a night." "You think it's going to be all night?" Marni asked angrily.

"No, no. They're taking the serious cases first. I heard two doctors talking. They have a few heart attacks, one car accident that looks bad. This is small potatoes. They'll probably send nurses out to patch people up. That's what I heard the suit say." Dom pointed to a harried administrator, who was racing down the hall, a phone to his ear.

"You think?" Seth asked.

"Yeah, they're gonna want to move these people," Dom repeated.

"See you in a couple hours. Hey, before you leave, you think you could buy a couple candy bars for us."

"Sure," Seth said. He went to the cafeteria and got on a line for the candy machines. He stood behind two men, a mulatto security guard and a very blonde EMT.

"You got any change, Chet?"

Chet shook his head. "I just have enough to buy fat bastard a Snickers."

"That's what you call Ralphie?" the blonde laughed. He had a lazy way of talking. Seth listened into their conversation. He couldn't place the accent.

"That or rat bastard. Depends on what he's making me do."

"You're funny," the blonde turned around to Seth. "Hey dude, change a twenty?"

Seth dug into his pocket. "How much do you need?"

"Change of twenty. I'm short a dollar for the rip-off machine."

Seth shook his head. "If you wait, I'll see how much I have left. You see that couple over there?" Seth pointed to his friends who looked like a couple of homeless people. "You think you could get them seen?"

The blonde took an appraising look at them. "I can talk to somebody."

"Greeeeat!!! Pick your snacks guys, it's on me." Seth used up all forty dollars on snacks for everyone, including licorice whips for his wife.

Dominic was seen in record time.

The EMT was from California, Seth smirked knowingly. He'd know that laconic accent anywhere.

*   *   *

"Man, you are lucky to be alive," Seth said from behind the camera. "Lemme see."

The foursome sat at the kitchen table. It was getting dark outside. While it seemed like it took forever, they were only in the hospital for three hours. The emergency room was getting packed, and Dominic just had a gash. The doctor had more important things to tend to, so they sanitized it and sewed it up one-two-three and sent him home.

Horror stories started to surface about young children and elderly people being attacked by cicadas. Even the nurses seemed to be getting more nervous. There were more stories about cicadas landing on cars and causing accidents.

"Four stitches and back in business, yo." Looking like Frankenstein's monster, Dominic's stomach was a patchwork. He started calling it a war wound and was admiring his ripped abs which were now red and swollen.

"Don't touch it, you moron," Marni warned. "It could

get infected. And turn off that stupid camera, Seth." She was clearly out of patience.

"Is it hot in here?" Lara said, sweating. Seth touched the air-conditioning vents. "It's on, but it's not cold. I'll check the thermostat."

His voice floated from the other room. "It's clicking on, but it's definitely not cool in the house." He came back to the kitchen where they were all having a midnight snack. "I'll go out tomorrow and check the freon. It's too late for anything now."

"It's going to be an oven in here tonight," Dominic complained.

"Turn on the news," Lara interrupted. "Let's find out what's happening in the area. That waiting room was pretty active."

"Lara, let's go to bed. Everyone's overreacting.

The doctors were great. I didn't see any panic, just a lot of insect-bite drama. By tomorrow they'll figure out something to exterminate the buggers and onto the next doomsday scenario."

"I want to watch the news," Lara insisted. "And I want to spoon," he laughed. "Seth one, channel four nothing." Then over his shoulder he told the others, "Spooning always gets 'em. Lights out, everybody."

* * *

The camera was charging on Seth's nightstand.

Night vision lit the room.

Seth was snoring the sleep of the exhausted, his

breathing loud and long. Lara turned uncomfortably from one side to the other. She was in a light sleep, hot, bulky, and miserable.

The room was still.

An AC vent swung open making a low squeak but not loud enough to wake Lara or Seth.

A gaggle of cicada poured out. Sheet rock and dust trickled down after them. A four-inch-long cicada crawled halfway through, falling onto the comforter at the edge of the bed. One by one, more cicadas followed the bigger one, dispersing around the room. Monstrously big, it climbed stealthily, working its way up Seth's long body, coming to rest near his mouth.

Seth snorted and batted at the annoyance, without quite waking up. The cicada's swordlike ovipositor poked down and aimed for his sweaty neck.

Seth's eyes snapped open. The scream died in his throat as he stared eyeball to eyeball with the insect. The cicada gently started rattling, making Seth jump into action. Attaching itself with the tenacity of a burr, it latched onto Seth's exposed skin.

The commotion stirred Lara out of bed, and she saw her husband wrestling with the bug. At first she thought it was a pillow and Seth was playing a joke. But Seth's scream shook her fully awake. It was a muffled sound because the cicada was blocking his windpipe with its ovipositor.

After her eyes adjusted, she saw the transparent wings. Letting out a shrill scream that would deafen a dog, it set off all the cicadas rattling in the room.

The commotion scared the bug, which naturally gripped harder. This woke Marni and Dominic, who burst into the room.

Seth rolled off the bed attempting to pull off the bug, and it tensed up even more.

"Help him!" Lara wailed, holding her protruding belly. Dominic, feeling none too spry himself, held his own midsection, too weak or too scared to help.

Marni grabbed everything from Lara's dressing table and started throwing it at Seth.

"Not the powder, stupid! Get a knife or something!" Seth said in a garbled voice. Marni ran out.

Seth barged his way into the bathroom using his shoulders. The gentle rattle of the cicadas turned into a symphony in the bedroom. Shrieking, Lara started swatting them with her shoes. The familiar summer sound filled the room.

"Seth." She stepped around the cicada carcasses, trying to make her way to the bathroom.

Nauseous and getting excruciating stomach pains, Dominic sank to the floor with a moan. Struggling to get off the floor, Dominic blocked the entry to the bathroom. He couldn't seem to muster enough energy to help Seth.

They heard the shatter of glass and muffled cursing coming from the bathroom. Lara stepped over the prone Dominic and lumbered to the bathroom door. Holding her slipper, slowly opening the door, she heard Seth curse,

"That'll teach you to sting, motherfucker."

Seth emerged holding a decapitated cicada by the foot. His neck was irritated from the bug's leg.

He looked at her flimsy slipper, "A slipper, Lara? Really?"

"I killed a few of them," she replied defensively. "Did it hurt you?"

Marni rushed into the room, brandishing Seth's baseball bat. Taking in their flushed appearance, he bowed elegantly. "I'd like to thank the Academy."

They all climbed onto the king-size bed. Seth was out of breath, Marni dazed. White with fright, Lara stroked her belly. Dominic was sick to his stomach. Spread around them was the carnage of their first battle.

"How'd they get in here?" Lara looked around the room. Marni pointed to the open vent.

They both shrieked.

Seth stood, stretching up with the bat to try to close the loose vent cover but couldn't reach it.

Dragging over an ottoman, he climbed up and banged the vent closed.

Seth started crushing the cicadas with his bare feet.

"What are we supposed to do?" Marni asked sheepishly. "Close all the AC vents? It's the middle of summer. We'll cook."

"I have some plywood in the garage." He looked at his nervous wife. "I'll drill them on. Dom, turn on the TV. Let's see what's going on."

Dominic picked up the remote and tried to turn on the television. Nothing but snow stared back at them.

"Here, give it to me." Seth held out his hand. He pressed buttons, clearly getting frustrated.

"It won't work any faster by you pressing the buttons, Seth. It doesn't work!" Marni offered snidely.

"Shut up, Marni!" Seth shouted.

Dominic slowly stood up. "Do you think cable's out?"

"Maybe you didn't pay your bill." Marni was still smarting from being yelled at.

"You know," Seth looked at her holding up his other hand, his thumb and index finger ever so close together. "I was this close to almost liking you." He then flipped her the finger.

"Screw you too, Seth," she flounced from the room.

"Marn…" Lara, ever the peacemaker, called after her.

"Just leave her, she can't go anywhere. Listen." Seth shut off the television. The gentle sound of cicadas outside had turned into a roar.

* * *

The next morning Seth was in the den documenting with the camcorder how he sealed off all the vents. He peeked in the living room where Lara, Marni, and Dominic slept on the floor, blankets. All the AC vents had been sealed off with plywood. Seth wasn't going through that again.

Deep down he was scared, but he wasn't going to show them. He decided to be a man of action. There was no way the bugs were getting into this house.

The AC vents were easy to seal.

He turned on the TV to see if he could find out anything else. Surely they weren't going to show daytime television. There had to be some type of additional coverage.

The TV picture was fuzzy but watchable now.

"Channel Five's round-the-clock coverage of the Great Cicada Invasion continues."

Seth chuckled to himself, "They'll name anything."

"The Northeast," the reporter continued, "is now engaged in an air war against the emerging cicada. Beginning this morning, aircraft are flying at three hundred feet, spraying a cicada-control product."

"It's about time," Seth thought. On the bottom of the screen, a Red Alert scrolled constantly warning people to stay off the streets. It was against the law to be outside.

Ted was interviewing "cicada expert" Dr. Benjamin Hawkner in a remote location. It was definitely not in the Northeast.

"It will kill the first wave," said the doctor. "What does the Center of Disease Control and

Prevention report?" Ted probed.

"The federal CDC reports that as of Tuesday there have been more than a thousand cases of cicadas attacking humans in the Northeast—New Jersey, 701 injuries, 22 deaths; Connecticut, 534

injuries, 12 deaths; New York, 336 injuries, 26 deaths, 9 on Long Island. Pennsylvania is the second most affected state. New York has been not affected too badly."

"Affected?" Seth said a little louder than he should. He didn't want to wake the others, but he was completely flabbergasted that they weren't saying how they were going to stop this.

Ted was now interviewing Dr. William Colon. "Has this spray been used before?" he asked.

"This has been used very, very carefully in many parts of the country," said Dr. Colon.

"William Colon chairs the Department of Preventative Medicine at Vanderbilt University Medical Center in Nashville, Tennessee," reported Ted.

"Is the spray safe?"

"Yes, but we're taking all precautions into account."

Ted was back in the newsroom. "Still, health officials are urging everyone to remain indoors over the next twenty-four to forty-eight hours until the spray has dried, especially pregnant women, elderly people, children, and pets. Furthermore, the Governor has declared a state of emergency."

"I cannot have any more deaths on my conscience because we did not take appropriate action," an exhausted Governor Goodman spoke into the camera.

He stood on a podium and addressed a forest of microphones. There was a burst of static, and the picture failed, but Seth could still hear his voice.

"There is no need to panic. The CDC is doing everything in its power to prevent further incidents."

"Governor Goodman, Governor…" Seth could hear all the reporters calling out to be noticed.

Seth turned off the TV. He didn't want to hear it anymore.

He moved to the kitchen and pulled open the shades. Cicadas were scattered all over the deck and backyard.

They were more prominent now. They seemed to multiply overnight. Seth shook the screen and the cicadas dispersed. The backyard was a mess.

The sudden drones of low-flying planes shook the foundation of the house. This scared the shit out of both Seth and the cicadas.

Peeking up, Seth saw a plane fly slowly overhead. It looked so low Seth thought he could reach out and touch it.

The buzz of more planes flying up above sounded again, coupled with a light dusting of grayish matter raining down.

Some of the bugs started to move crazily in circles.

"Government one, roach festival zero! Woo- hoo!"

Lara emerged from the doorway of the kitchen, staring sleepily outside. "Seth! What was that loud noise?"

She noticed the thousands of cicadas carpeting their backyard. Cupping her hands over her mouth, she stifled a scream.

"Seth!" a terrified Lara said. "They're everywhere! What are we going to do!?"

"Gives new meaning to the term 'snow day,' doesn't it?"

"What? What is going on?"

"They're spraying Raid on these cock-a-roaches," he calmly reassured her, as if it was his idea.

"Stop teasing, Seth!" "They'll all be dead soon." "How do you know?"

"Some idiot doctor on TV just said it," he retorted. He looked toward the backyard as more planes dusted the property.

"Close the screen!" said Lara. "I don't want to breathe that."

"Wanna go swimming?" Seth said nonchalantly as he obliged his wife's orders.

Marni entered the kitchen bleary-eyed. "Dominic isn't well," she said. She noticed the swarm in the backyard. "OH. MY. GOD!"

Another plane flew overhead. Marni ducked. "That sounds low."

"Don't worry, Marni. As tall as you are, it won't be hitting your head."

"I think we made it out of this," Lara said tearfully.

"We need to do something about Dominic," Marni stated. "He's really pale."

"We can't do anything now. Have to stay inside," Seth responded.

"Says who?"

"Elvis. He spoke to me last night. Who do you think? The news reports just said it on TV."

"Really?"

"Yes, really. You're stuck with me another twenty-four to forty-eight hours."

The three of them moved to the living room.

Dominic was lying, shivering, curled up in a blanket. Marni leaned in and touched his sweaty forehead.

"He's burning up."

"I'll get a thermometer," Lara said as she jumped to the next room.

"You OK, baby?" Marni softly asked Dominic. "I'm, I'm so cold," he said, shivering.

"You have an infection," said Marni.

"Can't go anywhere yet, buddy," interjected Seth. "Tomorrow we'll be able to take you to the doctor. They're spraying junk outdoors."

"That noise?" said a confused Dominic. "It's loud."

"It's the cicadas outside," Marni reassured him. "No, no. It's loud. It's humming."

"Those are the planes spraying insecticide," Seth said.

Marni gazed up at Seth. Lara returned with the thermometer. Marni stuck it in Dom's mouth; it beeped three times. "104. 2," Marni read.

"How about a drink, Dom?" Seth asked.

Dom shook his head an emphatic "no" and fell back asleep.

"I can't stay here," said Lara. "What if he's contagious? I shouldn't be near him."

"Don't worry. You both go upstairs. I'll take care of him." Marni never even looked up. "Do what you need to do today."

* * *

Seth and Lara peered through windows covered with insect parts. Dominic laid on the floor, his face as green as the area rug.

"I'm cold here, Marni. Get me a blanket," Dom muttered.

Seth placed his arm protectively around Lara. "Look, it's the garbage men. See, I told you nothing would stop them. Neither rain nor snow or…"

"That's letter carriers, stupid," Marni said over her shoulder, lugging Lara's new down comforter.

"Whatever, it's Oyster Bay's finest." "That's the cops, Seth," Marni croaked.

"All right already. It doesn't matter. They are here, and they're gonna help us all out," Seth told them, relief evident in his voice.

"See," he pointed to four burly sanitation workers wading through the piles of dead insects to the house across the street.

"Tell them we need them more." Lara tapped on the window, trying to get their attention. One of them waved to her.

She smiled graciously back and motioned at the worker to come to them.

The garbage man turned to say something to one of the others, who shrugged. One emphatically shook his head "no," and it looked like a rather heated argument ensued.

Finally, the one in command waved his arm in resignation, and the lone worker started to cross the street.

Suddenly he stopped dead in his tracks and looked wildly around. The others rushed for the safety of Jeff's house. They waved their arms and clearly were motioning the sole sanitation man to hurry. It seemed like the air went completely still, and Lara screamed as a wave of insects attacked their would-be savior. He writhed, falling into a heap of bugs, and they watched in horror as he seemed to disappear.

Seth pulled Lara against him, shielding her eyes while she sobbed. Marni stood next to them, frozen with horror.

A fierce battle ensued outside between the crew of workers as one tried to break off from the group to save his fallen comrade. The others held him back, the boss finally clipping the coworker on his chin, knocking him out. They dragged him quickly into Jeff's house.

The mound that was a kindly garbage man slowly stopped moving, and it was still as a tomb outside.

Seth whispered into Lara's hair, "We are screwed."

* * *

Seth made his way to the garage and got into his car, turning on the car radio, but not the vehicle. He didn't want to alarm Lara so he figured he would turn to his only credible source.

"Let's see what Bobby has to say about this," as he scanned for the station.

Bobby's garbled voice filled the speakers, no longer jolly and nonchalant, he sounded nervous.

"Last day for deliveries was yesterday," Bobby reported angrily. "We are cut off from the rest of the country!"

Michelle's throaty voice replied, "I don't understand why."

"The trucking companies are afraid to send their vehicles here and get trapped. All public transportation has been stopped. No airplanes, trains or ships. It's crazy! Did you see those gas lines today?"

"I had enough fuel to get here," Michelle replied.

"But I don't have enough to go home. Looks like you're stuck with me, listeners."

"Well I sure as hell am not deserting my fans. I don't understand why we don't have gas. The tankers are sitting in the harbor and our good-for- nothing governor won't release the shipments to be delivered. No deliveries. No fuel. No one can leave. We are trapped Long Islanders."

Seth glanced at his gas tank and saw that he was a little less than half a tank. He knew he should have gassed up before all this happened, but it was too late now. He wasn't leaving Lara alone. He felt that if he really had to get everyone out of the house, it should be enough.

"Not to mention the grocery stores are not being restocked," said Michelle. "What are people with children doing? What about the elderly? What about the handicapped? What about hospitals?"

"Hold on Michelle!" Bobby stopped her. "This just in. This is it. We are now under Martial Law. The National Guard is in charge and everyone is ordered off the streets. I don't believe this is happening here. This is a nightmare."

Seth punched the radio knob disgusted. He went back into the house.

*　*　*

Later in the evening, Seth and Lara were in their bedroom. He had spent the better part of the last hour helping her getting all the bug parts off the carpet. Putting the vacuum cleaner in the corner of the room, he said, "That wasn't a bad cleanup."

After washing up, Lara was trying to squeeze into a light summer dress she purchased when she found out she was pregnant. She was thinking about life after the Great Cicada Invasion.

"We'll recover really quickly, don't cha think? America always bounces back."

Seth averted his eyes and never mentioned a word about what Bobby said on the radio. "Sure baby. This is a cakewalk."

She looked at herself in the mirror. Seth filmed her huge belly.

"I'm really sad," Lara said.

Alarmed, Seth took in her large stomach and thought, "Wow, she really popped. Could be tomorrow, next day, day after that," Seth wondered pensively. Trying to change the subject, "Enough about being sad. Let's talk about something else. Where's that book that Jimmy's mom gave you?"

Lara turned to him with an incredulous face. "You mean the childbirth book? What would you need that for?"

"I don't know, just wanted some reading material tonight."

"If they're spraying outside, we're gonna get out of this. You're taking me to the hospital if we have to go. Right?"

"Of course we'll get to the hospital. I haven't let you down yet," Seth said reassuringly. "I just want to look at the book."

Satisfied with Seth's response, Lara said nervously, "I'm scared about Dominic."

"He'll be fine. He's gotten bugs before." "He looked ill. Stop teasing, Seth."

"The only thing you have to fear is…fear itself," Seth said seriously.

And with that, the power went out in the house.

CHAPTER 8
ISOLATION

"Stretch out your hand toward the sky so that the darkness can be felt."

- Exodus 10:21-23

THE ROAR OF cicadas was the loudest it had ever been. For a minute, Lara thought the power would pop right back on. Her faced glowed in night vision. Seth turned on the camera flash. It lit up the room with a big bright circle. Outside of that circle was total darkness. He handed the camera to Lara who followed him to the bedroom drapes.

Seth ripped open the shades to find the entire surface of the outside was a crawling mass of cicadas. Everything was covered. They couldn't distinguish anything.

A new plague had arrived, and Seth briefly wondered if they were going to survive this. The entire world would be talking about the great cicada emergence for centuries to come.

"We have to keep documenting this for as long as the camera has juice." He was glad he bought extra batteries just for the camcorder.

"What are we going to do?" Lara said frantically.

Seth grabbed the TV remote in the stupid hope that the TV would work. He slapped the remote a few times. He approached the TV and tried manually. Nothing.

"This is horrible." Lara gulped a huge sob.

The world was upside down. Moments before they lost power they were talking about the birth of their baby. Now they were stuck. Seth had to come up with a plan. Surely Google would have some info with whatever battery life was left in his laptop.

Seth slapped himself on his forehead and muttered, "What am I thinking? No power means no Wi-Fi."

He dashed out of the room and jetted downstairs.

"Seth!" yelled Lara. "Seth! Where are you going?"

Lara followed him. Marni exited her room groggy from the deep sleep.

"What's with the screaming?"

"The cicadas," said Lara. "They've covered everything. They've covered the entire house."

"No way. They sprayed them." "Where's Dominic?"

"He fell asleep downstairs."

Lara pressed past Marni to find Seth downstairs.

He was sitting in the den with his cell phone

illuminating his face. His fingers glided over the face of the phone rapidly.

"What's happening?" Lara moaned. "I don't know."

"Put on the TV," urged Marni. "Can't," Seth snapped. "Why?"

"Because the cicadas are covering everything, so get lost, Marni!"

"Don't get mad at me!" Marni turned her attention to Lara. "Call the police."

"Don't call the police," Seth interjected. "Call the power company." He turned to his wife. "See how long until we get back up."

Seth went back upstairs, leaving the girls alone. Lara handed Marni the camera to shine light on the landline.

"We should call the cops, Lara."

Lara sat looking at the phone like it was a ghost.

She didn't want to pick it up fearing what was on the other end.

"Do it," Marni insisted.

Lara hesitantly and slowly picked up the receiver. It was the loudest sound of silence she had ever heard. She clicked the receiver a few times.

She shook her head slowly at Marni. Landlines were becoming passé. Nobody even used them anymore. It was just a backup in case the cell phones were out.

"Where's your cell?" asked Lara.

Lara was moving upstairs with Marni in tow. Seth was pacing back and forth in the hallway. Sweat was dripping from his hairline. It felt like a sauna in the house.

"It has to be one hundred degrees in here. Did you get through?" asked Lara.

Seth didn't answer.

"Did you get through?" Lara tried again.

"Shut up for a minute!" Seth said abruptly. Marni felt more threatened than Lara.

Civilization was breaking down. "Don't talk to her like that!"

Seth wound up his arm holding his cell phone like a pitcher and launched it against the wall. The cell shattered easily. Breathing heavy like a madman, he barged his way downstairs.

"Where are you going?" Lara asked.

Seth didn't answer.

"Forget him," said Marni. "My cell is in the guest room."

Lara and Marni entered the guest bedroom. The covers were a mess. The room had the smell of decay. Lara wondered what her friends had been doing in there.

Lara went around to the side table and started typing on Marni's phone.

"What?"

Lara was sobbing and shaking. She held the phone up to the camera. "NO SIGNAL."

Marni was speechless.

"What are we supposed to do?" Lara said with her teeth chattering. It was still brutally hot in the house, but that didn't stop the chill going down her spine.

Marni came up with the best excuse she could.

"I...I have terrible service to begin with. That thing won't make a call in the City. Where's your cell phone?"

Lara moved to the master bedroom. The flash on the camera lit up the whole room. Lara picked up her cell phone from the side table. She slowly sat on the bed looking at the monitor.

"This is ridiculous." "Do you have service?"

"It isn't even searching for a signal!" "Connect to Wi-Fi."

Lara tapped the flat screen. She briefly wished she had her BlackBerry. She hated touching a flat screen. You didn't feel anything. With a BlackBerry, it felt like you were touching and getting results.

Her shoulders slouched. The answer was clear.

She held up her cell to Marni. "NO WI-FI AVAILABLE."

"No," Lara started breaking down. "No! This is not happening."

"Where are your flashlights?"

Lara opened the side table and rummaged through trinkets. Removing a flashlight, she remembered the last time she had turned it on— nearly half a decade ago when she moved into the house and power hadn't been turned on yet. It was dull. She remembered that she should have changed the batteries. The light slowly faded out.

"Oh no," Lara said.

"I'm glad he changed the batteries," Marni said sarcastically.

Lara was defeated. "Don't blame Seth. It's my fault too. Just leave the camera flash on. It's fully charged."

*　*　*

Seth entered the kitchen from the garage door entrance. "Car radio doesn't work. Static."

He approached Lara who was standing still and scared in the middle of the kitchen. He was at a loss for words. Feeling responsible, he closed his arms protectively around her.

"Guess the spray worked well, huh, Seth?" Marni acidly informed him.

This lit the fire that had been brewing from day one. Seth had had enough of Marni's snide comments.

"Why don't you pull down your pants? Your genital warts will surely scare them off."

Lara was shocked those words could actually come from Seth's mouth. "Seth."

"Now shut up and let me think," he topped it off.

"You dick," Marni said softly, but with enough venom it could kill a small bird. She said the next best thing she could think of directed to Lara.

"Why did you even marry this loser anyway? He can't even hold a job."

"Same deal with you, Marnes," Seth was not going down lightly. "I go through jobs like you go through guys."

"You are unbelievable."

"Funny, Dominic didn't say that about you." "What?" Marni asked incredulously behind the camera.

Marni leaned over to the kitchen table and fingered the picnic utensils tray they had left out. She didn't have a good pitching arm, so she threw it in the most hard-ass girly manner she could. It didn't matter; once the tray hit Seth the impact blasted plastic utensils around the kitchen area. At impact Seth slowly moved his head away unfazed. His body stayed still. The plastic knives and forks were scattered all over the floor.

"Enough!" Lara shouted, playing referee. "Enough, you two! Don't we have enough to worry about?"

"Get out!" Seth said quietly to Marni.

"Maybe you should leave," Marni said behind clenched teeth.

"This is my fucking house! You leave!"

Lara had to do something or Seth was going to explode. Marni was touching buttons that were fast approaching Defcon five.

"OK, listen," she started. "We have to check on Dominic."

Lara pushed Marni out of the kitchen. Seth was left standing in a disintegrating rage. Maybe he should throw Marni outside with the cicadas and let her nag them to death.

In the living room, Dominic was quaking. "Dom!" Marni shouted. "Dom! Can you hear me?"

"I…I'm…gonna puke."

Dominic leaned over and let up a sour bile tinged with brown. It was a bloody brown.

Something inside him was hemorrhaging.

"Seth!" Lara cried. "It's Dominic! Come here, something's really wrong."

Seth rushed into the room.

"Dom!" Marni knew this wasn't good, but there was nowhere she could take him.

"I can't breathe," Dominic said, choking on his own vomit.

She sat him up and patted him on his back.

Marni dragged over an ottoman for him to lean on. His color returned and he whispered, "Water."

The girls looked up at Seth as he barked out several orders.

"Give him some room. Let him breath. We gotta find some water. Marni, get him a piece of bread. Lara get him a glass of water."

Both girls sprang into action and rushed to the kitchen. Scarcely a minute later, Seth heard the groan of pipes and Lara's high-pitched call from the other room, "The water isn't working!"

"What?" Seth shouted.

Seth crouched and patted Dom on his shoulder. "You look better already dude. I'm gonna go get you some water. Call if you need me."

Seth was getting more nervous by the second. He dashed into the kitchen. Lara was going through the cabinets looking for the extra water Jimmy provided.

"Seth, where did you put that water Jimmy gave you?"

"What?"

He started playing with the sink faucet. The water groaned and clanked. A trickle of brownish, brackish water dripped down.

Lara screamed, "I know how to work a faucet! There is no water! It's not working!"

Seth wasn't listening. He parted the shade of the window over the sink. Marni moved woodenly over to the shade to stand beside him.

It was like a scene from the Bible. They were all different sizes, ranging from miniscule upward to four inches.

They were dangling from rooftops, crawling onto cars. Homes looked like beehives.

The streets were obliterated. Heavy with bugs, phone lines were drooping from the poles.

"Oh my God," Seth said it. Marni thought it. "Listen," Seth reasoned. "They pumped him full of antibiotics. He looks like he's got a hangover. You don't know if it's from the bite or…"

"When you visited Jimmy," Lara interrupted, "he gave you a box of water. We're out. Dominic should be drinking. In fact, I don't think I drank enough tonight either."

Seth was absorbed in the scene outside. "Water," he murmured, remembering how he first refused the offer of an extra water supply.

"How many do you have left?" Lara pressed. "I left it in the pantry in the laundry room."

Marni interrupted, "Um, were they blue packets called Emergency Water? I think Dom and I finished them a couple days ago."

Seth turned to her, his face a mask of rage, "How dare you! You, you, you thoughtless bitch!"

"I'm sorry!" Marni pleaded, her face drained of all color, her eyes imploring, "I am so sorry Seth. I never thought… can we fight about this later please. I'm scared Seth."

Seth's anger deflated like a spent balloon and suddenly he realized nothing mattered anymore. He had to find a solution to this madness. He had to protect his family.

"Try the bathroom," he ordered.

They ran to the bathroom, but Seth already knew what

he was going to find. "They've clogged the water," he said, watching the sluggish drip from the sink. "Don't flush; let's use just one of the bathrooms. Everybody use the one on the lowest level of the house."

"It's going to stink," Marni offered.

"No shit, Sherlock," Seth replied grimly.

Lara moved next to Seth. She scratched her belly and then wrapped her arms around herself protectively. "I'm getting really scared."

Dominic was on the floor, his face bleached of all color. His body rattled, hitting the wooden floor in a seizure. Lara grabbed a blanket from a closet. She got on her knees next to Marni. "Help me wrap him up, Marni," she demanded. "Help me wrap him up."

Seth crouched down. "I'll get him on the couch."

"What are we going to do?" Marni wailed. "They've ordered everybody to stay put." Seth

looked straight into Marni's face. "Who said that?" Marni shrieked.

"Do you want to know before or after I get him on the couch? Marni, he's lying in a pool of puke. Man, Dominic," he hefted Dominic onto one shoulder. "Seriously, dude, couldn't you have made it to the bathroom?"

"Seth!" Marni snapped.

"I'm only trying to lighten the mood." When she left, Seth turned to Lara. "This is bad. He should be in a hospital, but I don't want to take you out there, and I'm not going to leave you alone."

Lara didn't want to be left alone either. "We need the

car for the baby and me," she whispered, sweat dotting her lips. She looked like a wet cat.

"I know. I know."

"What are we going to do for water?" Marni called out, clearly at the end of her rope.

"You should have thought about that before you finished our emergency supply," Seth shot back. "Use the toilet."

"Seth, I don't think I can drink toilet water," remarked Lara.

"Well, we're gonna find out." Seth said as he laid a limp Dominic on the couch.

Seth moved to the front hallway bathroom.

"Something smells awful here." Lara held her hand over her nose.

"I don't know what you're talking about." Seth looked at her queasy face. He then darted into the kitchen and grabbed some plastic cups sitting next to the now-defunct refrigerator.

His bare soles slid on a gooey stain coating the floor near the fridge. He went down hard on his ass cursing roundly.

"Seth, are you okay. What's all this?"

Seth pulled himself up, grabbed a dirty dish towel and wiped his sticky foot. A large brown puddle oozed from the door of his stainless-steel refrigerator. He could smell the odor that was bothering his wife's sensitive nose. Opening the door, they caught a stench of rotting food.

"Oh, I forgot to clean out the fridge when we lost power. I'm sorry. "

"Ugh, that smells." Marni stood in the entrance of the kitchen. "All that ice cream, gone."

"All that meat…" Seth looked sadly at the decaying garbage. "Get a bag Marni, we have to clean this up."

"I'll do the freezer in the basement," Lara told them sadly.

Seth shook his head. "Marni will do it. Right Marn…" he challenged her to refuse him, but she shook her head defeated.

"Can we please worry about the water first?" Marni pleaded. "I will clean as soon as the lights turn on."

Seth went back to the bathroom and furiously scooped up toilet water into each cup and put them side by side on the sink counter. Marni and Lara were horrified.

"Seth," said Lara. "Drink."

He held a cup out for Lara. She took it but couldn't muster up the courage to drink.

"Drink."

"Seth, how about…" Marni was trying to think of something. "It smells." "Here…watch."

Seth grabbed the cup and downed the water. He spit a little bit from the sides of his mouth and gagged a bit as it went down hard.

He was thirsty but not overly thirsty. He could have easily waited until the next morning for the water to be turned back on. He needed to show the girls, actually prove to the girls, that in a crisis situation, there would be nothing wrong with drinking toilet water.

The girls went still.

"Shouldn't we boil it to kill whatever bacteria could be in there?" said Marni.

"How? You want me to go out there and use the gas grill?" He pointed to the carpet of bugs outside. "The electric stovetop is not working. She has to drink. She could dehydrate. The doctor even said it."

"I think I would take dehydration over drinking this," Lara whined.

"Bottoms up," Seth said as he forced the cup up to Lara's mouth, who submissively drank the water. Marni followed suit.

Lara quickly held her nose as she downed the water. Marni still filmed with the camera while she sipped it. It was bad. The taste was metallic and uric.

"Ah, see," Seth said, trying to lighten the mood. "Wasn't that bad."

Lara tried to digest. She put the cup down on the bathroom sink. "Awful." She kneeled over the toilet.

"I think I'm sick," said Marni.

Just the comment made Lara even queasier. She pushed Seth out of the way and puked into the toilet. Marni flung the camera at Seth and puked with Lara.

"If anyone has a plan B, I'm open to suggestions," said Seth. "What are we going to do without water and with Dominic?"

Lara looked up from the toilet, green. "Let Jimmy take him to a hospital."

Seth smiled in agreement. "Not just a pretty face, my Lara. All I have to do is get to Jimmy's and have him use his tank of a car to get Dom to the hospital. And…" He wriggled his eyebrows feeling lighter. "Get us some extra water. I tell you, I won't even mind bringing Jimmy's mom back with me. I bet she's birthed a kid or two in the last hundred years."

They made their way out of the bathroom to the living room where Dominic lie half dead on the couch.

Seth spoke directly to Dominic in a reassuring tone. "I'm going to the neighbors to get help, Dom. We're gonna beat Brood Ten." Marni sat next to Dominic on the couch and held his unresponsive hand.

"I'll go with you," Lara volunteered.

"Not until pigs fly are you stepping one foot outside," Seth responded.

"How about when the Northeast becomes overrun with cicadas?" Lara shot back.

Her nausea was slowly passing. Solutions felt better than complaints.

"No." Marni slid off the couch. "I'll go."

"No, you'll stay here." He pointed to Lara. "And you'll stay with her. Here. Period."

The girls followed Seth out of the living room, the sound of cicadas loud in their ears.

"Man, that's so irritating!" Marni covered her ears with her hands.

"This is quiet. The news reports said they get more active during the day," Seth assured her.

"Listen, Seth." Marni grabbed his shirt. "I have to go with you. Two sets of hands are better than one."

"What about Lara and Dominic?"

"Lara is safer here than anywhere else. If something happens to you, you may need help. Aside from that, we have to document your bravery for..."

"Quentin."

"Quincy," Seth and Lara spoke at the same time and then giggled, tension easing.

"She's right," Seth answered. "Besides, she can help carry back supplies from Jimmy's.

"Tell him you insist his mother stay here with us," Lara added. "Safety in numbers, you know."

"Sure," responded Seth. "She can sleep with us in our bed."

"Wait a minute!" Lara screamed. "You can wear the wetsuits."

Seth responded, "What you talking about?" "You know, the wetsuits we picked up in the Bahamas. If they protected us from fish, the cicadas won't be able to penetrate them."

*　　*　　*

Dressed in wet suits, complete with scuba masks and Burberry mufflers around their necks, Marni and Seth made a comical pair.

"We look like fashionable lunatics," Seth remarked.

The scuba gear, remnants of their honeymoon, would allow them to wade through the sea of cicadas outside.

Lara came from the basement with two pairs of Ugg boots and commented, "You're going to broil, but you have to be covered. I think I have nylons." She rushed to her bedroom.

Seth moaned, "Are you ready, Tonto?" He turned to Marni.

"Who said you get to be the Lone Ranger?" "You look like a Tonto."

"Well, you sound like one," Marni spit back.

"Stop. Jimmy's house. Remember— water, Dominic, baby due."

"To infinity and beyond."

"I guess that means I'm Woody." Marni gave Lara a long look.

They stood at the doorway. Lara lit a candle so she wouldn't be completely in the dark.

"I feel like I'm about to go on a really scary roller coaster that I just simply don't want to go on," Marni murmured.

"You made the height requirement." "This is bad."

"Stay here then."

Marni took a long look at Seth, her brown eyes sad. "No, I can't let you do this alone."

They looked at the door and slowly opened it.

Cicadas covered the entire screen. The sound made them both recoil with alarm.

"Oh. My, God," whispered Marni.

You couldn't see anything past the front door. "We'll go slowly. You follow me. Don't make loud noises. If one lands on you, don't freak; just take it off. If a lot land on you, I can't help you."

Seth slowly opened the front screen not to wake the sleeping cicadas. He looked back at Lara and mouthed the words, "I love you."

Lara started to cry, tears tracking down the side of her face, and whispered back, "I love you too."

They slithered silently outside and closed the door behind them.

* * *

The summer night was pitilessly hot. It was mainly quiet except for the distant echoes of the trillions of cicadas covering the land. There were no signs of humans. It was a black lunar landscape; the cicadas covered every surface.

With each step, their legs were knee deep in insects. Cars were abandoned in the streets; power lines smoked. It looked like a movie set, and Seth admitted he underestimated the infestation. There were no streetlights, and power was out all over, but Seth could hear the distant thrum of a generator somewhere in the neighborhood. It was Jimmy's, Seth thought confidently. He expected the house to be lit up like Disneyland. But it wasn't.

Jimmy's house felt like it was miles away, and he heard his own breath noisily in his head. From the corner of his eye, he saw Marni recording the mess. The camera flash lit a narrow path.

Within minutes his feet were coated with the blood and guts of the insects. The cicadas beneath the living ones were dead from the spraying. The top layer, about a foot worth of bugs, were very much alive, and sleeping. It was like walking on a balance beam.

Seth positioned his footing very slowly hoping not to make any sudden movements to awake them. Thinking this only brought on the sudden snap of a twig that was below a foot of cicadas.

The sound was louder than he expected. A group of

the bugs flew away clumsily, bothered by their slumber being disturbed.

"I think I just shit my pants," he said softly.

His gorge rose to the back of his throat, and he tasted acid. "Maybe Jimmy will have Tums," he thought grimly.

Seth walked in front of Marni, the soft squish of the insects warm on his feet. He could hear her gagging.

"Make sure you get a picture of what's going on out here," Seth said in a breath.

"Why? You think you're gonna forget it?" Marni snapped back.

"No. I want to show Dom and Lara what they're missing."

Thinking he saw a pale oval of a face in the window across the street, he gave a wave, but he faintly saw only the drapes pulled back into place.

"Well," he thought indignantly, "I never liked them either."

Seth did expect to see some movement, like after a big blizzard. Usually his neighbors would be helping each other dig out. But this was weird, really weird. There was no sign of humanity. Well, just Marni and him, and he thought with a chuckle, at least one of them was human.

People were completely freaked out and staying to themselves. Who cares, it was just a bunch of bugs. Someone was going to have to clean it up eventually. Hopefully Congress wouldn't take a snooze when it came to providing relief. He wondered briefly if he had insurance coverage for this. If he didn't, it looked like a permanent home in Arizona for him. He shuddered at the thought of sharing space with his in-laws.

Continuing the pace, a dozen cicadas landed on Seth's side between his armpit and hip bone. The last time cicadas landed on a human it was Dominic, and they both knew how bad that turned out. Seth froze.

"Seth!" Marni hushed. "Don't move."

The cicadas fluttered and lazily went back to sleep on Seth. He reached around with his left hand and slowly picked each one off. He set each one down with the rest of the gently humming brood.

They both made their way up Jimmy's long and cluttered driveway. The bugs were hip deep here.

The cars were unrecognizable, completely blanketed with cicadas. Here and there a faint cheep of a lone bug called out. I mean, Seth wondered, where were all the birds? He looked up to the empty night sky as they neared the porch, and again he was surprised at how silent everything was. He moved the scarf from his mouth, "Jim?

Jimmy. Mrs. Cain? Hello… anybody home?"

A large cicada flew right onto Seth's back. This bug was awake, annoyed and ready to attack.

"Seth!" Marni screeched, hitting his shoulders. "What!" He ducked; she was really hurting him.

"Stop, Marni!"

"It's on your back!"

Now he felt the weight of something warm on his back. He pushed himself against the post of Jimmy's railing, hearing the satisfying crunch of the now-dead bug.

"Got you. It's not that bad, Marni. Just crush and repeat."

"Seth, please, let's get out of here quickly." Marni's eyes

and nose were running from behind the camera. She was clearly not an attractive crier.

Seth quietly brushed off smaller cicadas frozen on the creaky screen door. Oddly enough, the door to the house was ajar. He turned the camera flash into the darkened interior. Goosebumps moved up his spine, and Seth wondered why crazy Jimmy left the house open. "I wonder if there is an underground bunker somewhere under all the garbage," he thought.

They entered the kitchen; dust motes mixed with insect wings floated on the grayish air. It was foul in there. Marni gagged, and he heard her dinner making a return appearance in a messy corner of the kitchen.

"Stinks," she uttered thickly. "It sure does," Seth whispered.

"Jimmy," he called tentatively. They walked into the den; the place looked abandoned. "They must have cut out of here," Seth said as he tripped hard against something on the floor. It felt soft and hard at the same time, and for a minute Seth felt black dots floating before his eyes. It couldn't be, he thought, it just couldn't be. Feeling trapped in some bad science fiction movie, Marni moved the camera flash down to shine it on the decaying face of Jimmy. Seth was a mere inches from his face.

Seth heard screaming, and when he looked at Marni's horrified face, he realized they were both howling at the top of their lungs. This didn't happen in Oyster Bay. This couldn't be happening in America. This wasn't real. He wanted to wake up, now!

Marni clutched his shoulder and helped him up.

He screamed like a girl, he thought ashamedly.

"Seth, we have to get out of here," she told him breathlessly.

For the first time in thirty-two years, Seth was speechless. No sound came from his mouth. He worked his jaw but could find nothing to add, no pithy remark. He knew only he wanted to go home and be with his wife. For a scant second, he wouldn't have minded her father as well.

Reason returned. "Wait, Marni. We should find out if his mom is OK." He forced himself to relax and breathe deeply—well, not too deeply, but calmly.

"Are you kidding me?" she hissed.

"Well, she might be. And we've got to take some supplies. I'll check out the bedroom. You go back to the kitchen and see what's in the cabinets."

"I'm staying right next to you. What do you think happened to Jimmy? Did the bugs really eat him?"

"I guess he wasn't prepared for this," Seth said as he inched down the dark, hot corridor to the bedrooms.

How could anyone prepare for something like this? He wondered briefly about the family that ran to upstate New York where there were mosquitos bigger than helicopters, what could one expect from the cicadas.

He thought about extreme preppers and all their canned goods, and wondered who would outlast whom. String beans or the bugs? Are you feeding yourself just to be more food for the bugs or do you run? And furthermore, run where? Ultimately, he realized, you have to know what you're prepping for. Nobody in the world could have prepared for something as biblical as this.

Marni followed, feeling Jimmy was going to get up and pull a prank on them. She kept looking back at his feet in the living room. He was swollen and bloated, his shirt torn open. His body was covered with cicadas sticking their ovipositors into his flesh.

"Hello," Seth blurted out. "Hello. Ma'am. It's Seth Fletcher, your neighbor."

Nothing. Just the sound of cicadas scurrying up and down the hall with them.

Seth noticed an open door. "Shine the light in there."

Marni moved the camera to the door that was cracked open. Seth opened the door even further. It felt jammed until he realized he was moving a pile of those bugs with every inch he shoved open the door.

There she was. Lying on a bed in pitch darkness covered with those things. Their rattlesnake shrill echoed in the room. Seth gagged while Marni screamed. The room stank of rot.

Jimmy's mom was grossly overweight, but now she was even more swollen. There were bugs in her hair, on her face, underneath her nightgown.

Speechless, Seth stared back at the sightless eyes. "I don't believe this. Wake me, Marni." It was sickening to see.

Nothing mattered at this point. Seth knew he had to get the supplies, get whatever else he could, and get home to his wife.

The door creaked and some cicadas started flying around the room. Seth slammed the door shut, waking cicadas in the house. They started flying around, landing on them.

"Let's raid the supplies and get out of here." They made their way back into the kitchen, and after brushing off boxes against the wall, Seth asked Marni to take out the reusable shopping bags Lara had so thoughtfully packed. They stuffed them with water packets and canned goods.

"Should we take the tuna? You know how Lara feels about the mercury."

"Well, she'll just have to make do." Seth loaded the bag with whatever he could fit in it.

"I'm going into the basement. You stay up here." Seth grabbed the camera and galloped down the dark stairwell. "Keep talking to me so I know you're OK."

"Amazing grace, amazing grace…saved a wretch like me…"

Seth heard Marni's reedy voice eerily down the steps.

"Um, cheerful," he called back and started humming with her.

The bugs were not so overwhelming here, and in a backpack Seth stuffed bandages, antibiotics, a Swiss army knife and … "Hello, darling," Seth whispered as he took a Glock off the shelf. He grabbed ammo, hoping it fit the gun, and bounced up the steps two at a time.

"Let's blow this joint."

"Where are the cops?" Marni whimpered, holding Seth's hand as they walked through the carpet of insects. "Why isn't anyone helping us?"

Seth yanked her, walking as fast as he could. "I don't

know. I just know that prepping wasn't enough. Man, am I glad I didn't waste money on that."

Seth gave the camera back to Marni. They got to the front door. "Count of three. We open and go back."

"OK."

"One," Seth said.

"Two," Marni was hyperventilating.

"We are gonna die!" Marni howled. "All of us! We are dead. This is bad, really, really bad."

"Stop it," Seth shook her. "You have to be strong now, Marni. Lara and Dominic need us. Stop wigging out. I know you're stronger than this." "You do?"

"Yes, I know you took care of Lara in college. I may not respect the choices you made in life, but I respect you."

She hugged him hard. This very well could be their last hug.

"Are you ready?" Seth asked. Marni nodded her head. "Three."

They opened the door slowly. The cicadas were still sleeping outside. They made their trek back home, realizing they were in Jimmy's house longer than they should have been.

Seth passed the window to Jimmy's mother's room and noticed the glass was broken. The cicadas must have punched through the glass and gotten into her room.

As they waded through the bug muck, Seth felt something wrong with the air. If the weight of the cicadas could have broken the window, something worse was going to happen.

He glimpsed to his right. He wasn't psychic, but he only knew he had a great sense of foreboding. It was as crushing as the mountains of bugs outside. He hated that feeling. On the side of Jimmy's house was an enormous tree. It topped out at about thirty feet. That was on par for Oyster Bay. Trees were everywhere. That's why everyone's allergies were so bad during the springtime.

The tree was covered with cicadas. A large branch of the tree was starting to bend from the weight. It creaked and groaned with the weight of the heavy bugs. Seth didn't know if they could make it home in time.

Grabbing Marni's hand, he started running fast. The cicada looked about ready to awake and swarm both of them.

The tree branch bent lower until the pressure snapped the bark. The loud crack woke thousands of cicadas as they fluttered away from the tree and toward Seth and Marni.

"Run!" Seth yelled. He didn't care if he was going to wake the cicadas or not; he was not ending up like Jimmy.

Marni and Seth blasted off from the house, but running in knee-deep bugs was like running in a pool. The friction was too much, and the faster they wanted to go, the longer the route took. They had to get back into the house. Seth started thinking about the weight of the cicadas on the glass and the roof.

As Marni was trying to get through the mess, she tripped and landed face down on the glistening bugs. The cicada quickly scattered around her, engulfing every part of her body.

The camera was quickly covered with the sea of bugs.

Seth fired shots in the air. It was the first time he had

ever shot a gun in his life. It was so loud. He covered his ear with his shoulder. He didn't think, just reacted.

The cicadas scattered off Marni in all different directions. The wet suit had kept her safe. Seth was furiously dusting the remaining bugs off her.

She felt them poking.

Her backpack was protecting her back as well. It was heavy with all that water. Instead of dusting it off, Seth ripped it from her body. The cicadas swarmed the backpack. He dropped it in the mess.

She stumbled to her feet, snatched the camera off the ground, and ran with Seth to the house.

They made it to the porch. Seth fired at the cicadas hoping they would scatter, which they did. He kicked cicadas off the glass screen. Lara was standing there trembling.

Seth and Marni opened the door and fell inside. The door slammed behind them. Marni threw the camera on the hallway table.

They start rolling around the floor crushing whatever cicadas were stuck to their bodies.

As Marni rolled, tears poured down her face. "We're dead, we're so dead."

"Honey, I'm home," Seth called out as he rolled from side to side crushing the bugs.

Lara kneeled down next to him. "Tell me what to do. Are you hurt?"

"No."

"What happened?"

"We went for dinner. Saw a movie. It was a nice date,

right Marnes?" Seth packed the heat in the back of his jeans. "Use only in case of emergency."

Lara knew Seth was fine. If he was joking, he was fine.

"I was so worried about you," she said as she kissed him. "I've been holding Dom's hand. He's worse; he keeps getting worse. We have to give him some water." She was dirty and disheveled.

Marni had already stripped out of her dirty gear and got into her plaid pajama bottoms and t-shirt. She went to the living room and held Dom's head. Seth stripped down to his T-shirt and jogging pants.

"Where's the water?" asked Lara.

"There were too many cicadas," replied Seth. "What else did you get?"

"I got a gun."

"I heard the gunshots. That was you? Who were you shooting at?"

"Worst-case scenario, we can use it on ourselves."

This stopped everyone in the main foyer. Seth was joking, but they knew there was a hint of being serious. Was that their worst-case scenario, or had they just reached the worst-case scenario. Seth knew if the house wouldn't hold up and those bugs were destroying everything in their path, they would have to kill themselves or die a horrible death like Jimmy and his mother. Just thirty feet from his house lay Seth's dead neighbors. If it could happen to Jimmy, who prepped, it could happen to them.

Seth wasn't about to give up. "I'm just kidding. We'll never give up. Help has to come."

Marni was listening to Dom's chest. "He's barely breathing. Come on, honey, please sit up."

Seth took the camera and put it on the fireplace overlooking the living room. This way, everyone had light to see.

Dominic gave a gurgling cough and started shaking uncontrollably. Foaming from the mouth and convulsing, he started spewing vomit, which just missed Marni. He sat up frozen. Everyone held their breath.

He opened his eyes. "Dom!" shouted Marni.

Dominic didn't respond at all. His eyes rolled in the back of his head, and he collapsed backwards. His tense arms and knees were finally relaxed.

Everyone lost it. Marni started hitting Dom. Lara broke down in tears. Dominic couldn't be dead.

Seth bent over to open one eyelid. The pupils didn't respond. "I'm sorry, Marni. This is bad."

Marni shook his chest. "Dominic!"

"I don't believe this." Lara turned to Seth, stupefied. "What's happening to us?"

Seth took a blanket from the couch and covered Dominic's face. Marni fell to the floor, punching a couch cushion. Seth tried to console her, but she moved away.

The room fell silent. They were done for, and everyone knew it. Seth backed himself into a corner; Lara leaned up against him. Marni curled herself up in pain, sobbing over her dead boyfriend.

"We are grasshoppers," Seth began. "We are all grasshoppers."

"What are you talking about, Seth?" Lara looked at him.

"This ant, this little tiny ant went around the field collecting grains of wheat and barley so he could store up food for bad times. Well, a grasshopper watched the ant and laughed, laughed and laughed at the ant. 'Whatcha doing, li'l guy,' he asked? 'Getting prepared for hard times,' the ant responded without stopping his work. The grasshopper picked up a fiddle and started to sing the day away."

"Seth, stop," Lara moaned.

"This ant. He didn't pay any attention to the grasshopper and went about his business. When the harvest was washed away by rain, and the bad times came, the grasshopper got hungry. He went to the ant and begged for a bit of food."

"Your prepper was dead, Seth," Marni hissed. "What's your point?"

"Jimmy's dead?" Lara whispered, shocked.

"The ant replied, 'Oh, grasshopper, poor grasshopper. If you had done some work yourself instead of singing and making fun of me while I was hard at work, you wouldn't be asking me for food. '"

"What's your point? Dominic is dead; Jimmy is dead. His food is useless to both of them!" Marni screamed.

"The world is fiddling, and all the ants are dead," Seth replied tonelessly.

"I don't understand you."

"There are no cops because nobody ever believed something like this could happen. The world is made up of grasshoppers who think nothing is ever going to happen to them."

"What happens to the grasshopper in the story?" Lara asked in a small voice.

"The grasshopper dies," Marni said flatly.

Lara grabbed her belly and sobbed, tears dripping down her face.

Seth, caught up in his own misery, realized he was crying for the first time in his known life.

"I'm a grasshopper too," he wailed as his arms curled around Lara.

Lara sighed softly and became deadweight in his arms. "Lara!" he screamed.

Her eyes rolled back in her head as she clutched her stomach. Water poured down her legs.

CHAPTER 9
LABOR

"One is never afraid of the unknown; one is afraid of the known coming to an end."

- Jiddu Krishnamurti

"I NEED A kid now like I need a fucking hole in my head." Seth said as he ran to the bathroom and dipped a hand towel in the toilet. He went back to gently bathe Lara's pale face. She blinked and clutched her belly.

"You okay?" Seth asked her.

"Never better," she replied weakly with a smile. Marni gasped and cried out.

"Look at Dom!"

Dominic's body started twitching. Whatever fear the three had coursing through their veins would now be magnified by a billion. They all let out a blood curdling scream.

"He's alive!" yelled Seth. He grabbed the camera and approached Dom.

The girls scurried away on their butts as Seth slowly approached the covering draped over Dom's face.

Seth ripped off the cover. Dominic's eyes were wide and lifeless. His mouth was ajar but his body still moved.

"Dom," Seth said lightly. Dominic didn't respond. "Dom," Seth said louder.

Still nothing. Seth was thinking that Dom was going to spring up and say, "April Fools!"

Seth gave it all he got. "Dominic! Wake up!"

A cicada scurried from Dominic's mouth. Then another and another and another. They began pouring out of him by the dozens. The cicadas pushed their way out of Dominic and all over the living room floor. With every regurgitation of cicadas, Dominic moved like he was throwing up. The bugs had found a new host and were crawling from his stomach through his esophagus and out his mouth.

Seth turned around, grabbed the camera, and pushed Marni and Lara upstairs. He still needed time to think what they should do next.

Rushing up the stairs, the cicadas filled up the walls. He flung open the master bedroom door, then the bathroom door. He shoved Marni and Lara in the bathroom and followed. They all heard the scratching of the cicadas on the door and walls outside.

However loud it had been the past few days outside,

the house still muffled the rattlesnake sound. In the house it was deafening. Everyone had to shout.

They huddled on the floor, exhausted. It was almost morning, and they had all been awake for the past twenty-four hours.

Seth laid the camera on the counter. It was pointing directly at them.

Crawling over to Lara, who was lying flat on the floor in tremendous pain, he helped her sit up.

Her hair dangled in front of her face. She was breathing heavily, labor pains racking her. Seth rubbed her back gently.

"I did this," he said tearfully.

Marni started sobbing along with him.

Lara felt a contraction and started moaning. She flung herself back to Seth.

Even lying down, Lara was more uncomfortable than sitting up. She rose and started pacing the spacious bathroom.

Seth buried his head in his hands, hitting his forehead. He knew they had to get out of there.

No food, no water, no power, no cell service, no Dominic. He gazed up. No one had a clue what to do. He realized there were two options. One, they could stay in the bathroom until the room caved in from the weight of the bugs, or two, they could try their luck outdoors—well, Lara said babies bring good luck.

"Let's go," Seth said decisively. At first, no one reacted because they were all wrapped up in their own pain.

"Let's get out of here!" yelled Seth, startling the girls.

"What?" said Marni. "We're leaving."

Seth rose, taking as much of Lara's weight as possible. "It hurts."

"Come on," said Seth, "we're leaving." Hoisting her against his hip, he said, "We don't have a choice. If we stay here, the roof is going to cave. We have to try to get out of here."

"Where are we going?" said Marni.

"We're leaving. It's almost morning. Last night was nothing. The cicadas are more active during the day."

"And that is why we should stay here!" "We're gonna die here, Marni," Seth pleaded.

"We have to get her to a hospital."

Lara was doubled over. "We can't go outside." "Yes we can. We're getting in the SUV and we're getting you to the hospital."

"What about the cicadas that just took over your house?" asked Marni.

"My wife and baby are not dying." Seth was adamant. He grabbed a towel from the rack and draped it over Lara's shoulders. "Take the camera, Marni. Keep filming. My kid's gonna see this one day."

A heavy snapping sound surrounded them from above. There was cracking and creaking that sounded like two-by-four wood being snapped in half. Seth knew what it was, but he wouldn't tell anyone.

"What's that noise?" asked Lara. "Nothing. We have to move."

"It sounds like the house is collapsing," Marni shouted.

"Now! We have to go now. Go straight to the garage. Don't look back."

They heard glass cracking, a tinkle followed by a cascade

as the bathroom skylight collapsed under the weight of the bugs. The bugs rained down.

They opened the bathroom door, then the master bedroom door. Sunlight filtered in through the cicada-covered windows. As they entered the hallway, cicadas were everywhere. Not as bad as outside, but there was no exterminator in the world that was going to be able to fix this, Seth thought glumly. "Arizona, here we come."

Cicadas started leaping for the moving targets. Seth shot the gun as the cicadas tried to fly on Lara, Marni, and him. They came apart like an overripe watermelon, spilling guts and startling the other bugs.

They raced downstairs. They made it to the door to the garage and slammed it behind him.

"Lara, backseat. Marni, up front with me."

Lara lifted herself in and Marni entered on the passenger side. Inside the truck, Marni was filming them. "Lara, do you want me to sit with you?" Lara shook her head with an emphatic "no."

Seth flipped on the ignition. The SUV roared to life. "At least something works," Seth said grimly. "Lara, Lara baby, how are we doing?"

"Pain," whimpered Lara. "Lots. Of. Pain." "Keep breathing."

Seth blasted the air conditioning. "Aaaaah, air to breathe. Do you feel it, Lar?"

Lara was breathing, using the Lamaze technique. "The air is warm, but once I get us moving, it will cool down," he assured her.

Seth put the SUV in reverse, his hand over Marni's

headrest, and turned around. "Hold on!" He released the break and slammed on the gas. The rear bumper crashed into the garage door with a loud bang.

Lara squealed. The garage door didn't budge two inches. Throwing the car into drive, he gently pulled up as far as he could go. With the amount of space he had to work with, he was busting through this. "It's narrow, but I think I can break through," he said confidently.

He threw the car in reverse and slammed on the gas. A loud screech and a bang and this time it made a dent. He slammed his gear back to drive and plowed into some shelving he installed when they first moved in. He reversed again and even faster than before slamming into the garage door. The sides of the garage door separated from their rails. Sunlight streamed in. Cicadas start crawling in through the cracks.

"The cicadas are coming!" yelled Marni.

That was it. This was their last bastion. Now the cicadas were in every room of the house including the garage. There was no turning back. Either they were getting out of the garage or dying from carbon monoxide poisoning in their car.

Seth put the car into drive and crashed into the wall in front of him. He brought the shifter up to reverse. With his foot on the brake, he revved up the gas to eighty miles per hour. Releasing the brake, he took out the double garage door leaving a gaping wound in the face of his house.

"Yes!" screamed Seth as he sped down the driveway. Happiness turned to utter panic when he looked at his house from the street. "Well, that's a bitch of a repair."

Cicadas streamed into the house. The roof started collapsing.

"Not the house!" Lara moaned as she watched the home she loved collapse in on itself. There was nothing they could do.

Marni's car was an indistinguishable lump on the street that didn't even resemble a vehicle anymore.

He gunned the car in the direction of the highway. The tire tracks behind them left a pile of dead cicadas but quickly filled up with fresh ones.

Lara panted from the backseat, quickly forgetting about the destroyed home. "This really hurts."

"Breathe like Nurse Diesel told you." Seth was careening down the deserted streets. Cicadas blanketed homes. The landscape was dotted with destruction.

"I thought they sprayed these things to death," Marni choked out.

As if on cue, they heard the drone of airplanes dusting the area with more pesticides. They watched bluish flakes drift down coating everything like a blanket. "Looks like they changed the formula." Seth watched the cicadas start to react to the poison.

"What are you talking about?" Marni snapped. "It was gray before. Now it's blue," Lara

volunteered between pants. "You think it's OK to be breathing in this stuff?"

Both Seth and Marni turned incredulous faces to her. "What? I'm just saying," Lara shrugged.

The drone of the duster plane became a loud whine.

Marni pointed in front of them as they watched the plane hurdle crazily toward them.

"Seth!" she yelled. "Look out!"

Seth swerved onto a lawn as the plane smashed directly into the middle of the street. Flames shot out from the crushed engine.

"Another close call," said Seth as he dodged between abandoned cars laying at crazy angles, blocking the streets. Seth raced down one familiar street only to find broken trees cut off their way of escape.

"I can't believe this. You would think the government would have opened up the roads for emergencies like this," he said to no one in particular.

"I wonder if the power lines are live." Lara looked at the tangle of downed wires.

"Well," Seth responded," we're about to find out." He pressed the gas, squinted his eyes, and drove under a mass of lines. One hit the top of the truck, and they all gasped collectively.

"I guess power's out," Marni volunteered.

For some reason, Seth found that hilarious and started to shout with laughter. Lara and Marni soon followed, and they laughed so hard, tears streamed down their faces.

It was literally raining cicadas.

Seth put on his wipers and watched them scatter the bugs away from his windshield. It quickly became sticky with their blood, so he used the wiper fluid to clean his view.

"There is no help for this," Seth finally said. "I don't know why there is no National Guard taking care of this. This is biblical."

"I don't remember going this way to the hospital when we went with Dom," Marni's voice cracked.

Seth squinted through the mess of his windshield. Lara's contractions were getting worse. She screamed.

"Lara, you OK, baby?" said Seth.

She screamed even louder as she sprawled out on the backseat of the car. She was gripping the headrests so tight it was leaving an indent of her hand.

"Did it pass?" asked Marni. Lara shook her head no.

"Almost there," said Seth. "We're getting onto the highway now. Looks like they did clean the main roads a bit."

He noticed an abandoned car on the entrance to the highway ramp. He jerked the wheel forty-five degrees, narrowly missing it. Everyone swerved with the motion of the car.

"Contraction passed," Lara said with a sigh of relief.

"Good! Good! Hang on Lar."

"Seth?" Marni asked sheepishly. He didn't answer. "What if the hospital has no power?"

"They'll have power." "How can you be so sure?" "Keeping the faith."

Seth noticed a van heading in his direction. He veered hard right as a van came careening toward them, covered with cicadas. The world spun in a kaleidoscope of colors. Horns blared, and for a minute, everything was silent in the car.

Their car fishtailed due to the condition of the roads, which were slick with cicadas. No matter how hard Seth tried he couldn't gain control of the wheel.

There was a loud screeching sound as the SUV spun out, finally hitting the highway divider with a loud crash. The windows remained intact, but the car body was badly damaged.

After the crash the interior of the car went dark quickly. Cicadas settled gently over their car.

Silence surrounded them.

Seth was too shaken to move. He mustered any energy he could find and leaned forward to flip on the interior lighting. The wipers swiped at the bug- covered windshield. This brought in more light to the car.

"Everyone OK?" Seth asked, wiping his sweaty forehead.

"Help," Lara meekly said from the backseat. Seth turned to see Lara lying motionless on the SUV floor. She was bleeding from her forehead. At impact, Lara hit her head on the air conditioning vent in the back of the car.

Seth sprung off his seat and jumped in back. He lifted her by her shoulders back onto the seat, her head resting in his lap.

"It hurts so much, Seth. I don't think we're gonna make it."

"We're gonna make it. You're gonna be fine." Seth rubbed her forehead. He cleaned the blood off with his T-shirt. They both started to cry. "You're gonna be fine. I got you. I won't let anything bad happen to you. I promise."

Marni understood now. She understood everything Lara was telling her over the past few months. She knew how much Seth and Lara loved each other, and not even a national emergency was going to tear them apart. She wished she could find that same love with someone. She never felt that way about Dominic, but she had a newfound respect for her friends. For however long they were going to survive, there was no way she would pester her about Seth and his attitude ever again.

Seth attempted to get up, but Lara squeezed him tight.

"Please stay," she said through a well of tears. "I'm scared."

"Lara, I gotta get you to the hospital." "How do we even know there is a hospital? Please don't go, Seth; I can't take this! It hurts so much."

"Listen to me," he said. Lara opened her blue eyes and locked them with Seth's. He wiped her tears again now mixed with the blood from her face.

"I'm taking control."

A loud horn broke through the car like a shotgun.

"Seth!" yelled Marni. "No."

"It's headed right for us!" Marni wailed.

"No, no, no, no, no! Hold on!" Seth echoed throughout the car. He curled to cover Lara's head and chest. Marni gripped the armrest as tight as she could.

An out-of-control Mack truck was headed for them straight on. It bounced around the highway like a loose ball in a pinball machine. The driver must have gotten off the wrong exit and was heading east, while every other car was heading west.

It broke through cars like they were paper- mache. The truck was covered with cicadas. The window was completely blacked out from those bugs. "Why doesn't he clean them off with his wipers?" she wondered, watching the truck barreling toward them.

The wipers of Seth's SUV wiped away at the gathering bugs. The truck was flying down the highway and getting even closer.

"We're going to die," said Marni. "Don't look!" yelled Seth. "This is it."

"Marni, stop looking!"

Fifty feet away. Wipe. Forty feet away. Wipe. Thirty feet away. Wipe.

"Turn the wipers off, Marni," ordered Seth. "We won't feel anything."

A hysterical Marni leaned over and switched off the wipers. The bugs quickly filled up their view. They noticed that the bugs had started poking the glass.

The horn blared and sounded closer.

Seth was praying out loud. "Please forgive me. I am sorry. I am sorry for what I did to my family."

Marni was breathing in quick pants. Lara was actually wishing she was dead; the pain was too great.

The horn enveloped the entire car. It blared just to the right of Marni's window. She gripped harder. Seth clenched his teeth so hard he was afraid he was going to break them. It didn't matter at this point. The truck would turn them into a pile of dust in just a second.

The truck horn went right through the car and behind them. Seth unglued his eyes. A loud explosion was heard from behind. This blew the bugs off the back window.

Seth meekly turned around and saw an oil tanker spilled onto the side of the road in flames. Thick black plumes of smoke billowed from its tank.

"Are we dead?" asked Marni.

"I hope so," Lara said.

"Not by the hair of my chinny-chin-chin! Yes!"

He saw the destruction behind them. The truck missed them by inches, possibly centimeters. He briefly wondered if the driver even made it out of the wreckage alive.

Seth climbed over Lara and into the front seat of the car. "I guess we're not done yet. I'm gonna go for act two."

Seth tried to start the car; the engine groaned as the car shook and stalled. Taking a deep breath, his face red, Seth tried again and this time the car started. "Come on, come on." Success, no stalling. Seth winked to Lara and said confidently, "Let's get this show on the road." The car roared to life.

He flew down the highway dodging abandoned cars, wondering briefly if people were still in the vehicles. Prayers slipped from his agnostic lips, and he discovered his newfound piety comforting. They were going to make it. He had to get his wife to the hospital before the baby made his grand entrance.

"Here it comes again," said Lara.

"How far apart are you?" asked Marni. "It's close."

"How close?"

"Really close!" Lara roared from behind clenched teeth.

"It should just be a few more minutes," assured Seth.

"I can't take this anymore!" yelled Lara as she banged her fists against the headrest.

"If we survive this, I'm never having sex again," remarked Marni, looking at Lara's distressed face.

"It's here," Lara panted.

"We're almost there," Seth urged. "No, it's here!"

"What's here? What do you see?" Seth was looking outside for a clue, but all he saw was the infestation.

"Seth!"

"I think…" said Marni.

"Seth, the baby's coming," Lara wheezed. There was still five more miles to the hospital.

With the treacherous roads, there was simply no way he was going to get her there on time. Seth knew it was his time. It was his time to grow up.

Cool as a cucumber, and not fazed one iota, Seth slowly pulled the car over to the side of the road. He neatly put the car in park and turned to Marni. "Time to go to work."

He climbed in the backseat. Lara was a sweaty mess. In an attempt to calm her down, he joked, "Hi, Lara, how ya doin? Wanna get some sushi?"

Seth grabbed the towel that was thrown in the back, covering the seat. "Now listen to me," he ordered. "Rest your head on the window. Back up."

Lara scooted up. Seth reached up her dress and took off her panties. He threw them in the trunk of the car.

Feeling the urge to lift her legs, Lara kicked at Seth who accommodated her as best he could. "Move the seat forward, Marni." He continued issuing orders.

Seth thought furiously He spoke to himself in a rushed whisper. "What did the book say? What did the book say Breathe…before, the middle, no it was…what was that word?"

"The height!" he yelled out. "Lara, listen to me. Breathe at the height of pressure. Breathe hard and push when the contraction hurts the worst. We're gonna do this together. Come on, breathe, baby."

Sweat glistened on her face, and her mouth was stretched back in a tight grimace. Lara groaned a deep noise from her heart.

"I see his head! It's really happening. Just push, Lara. I'm here. Marni and I are here."

The cicadas were beginning to cover the car and block the light. "Shine the light from the camcorder, so I can see what I'm doing," he told Marni.

"I would think after all this time, you'd be very familiar with the area, Seth."

For the first time, Seth looked up and grinned at Marni. "You're not so bad, kid."

"Much as I am happy you two are bonding, this time can it be only about me?" Lara sniped.

Laughing, Seth instructed Lara, "Now breathe…hee, hoo, hee, hoo."

"Heeee, hoooo, heee…"

Marni couldn't help but breathe just like Lara. "Hee hee, hoo, hoo."

"Cut it out, Marni," he said.

"Do you see anything yet?" Marni asked. "Hemorrhoids," Seth looked up at Lara and

grinned. "You're doing great, honey." "Pressure, I feel so much pressure." "Push, Lara," Marni told her. "Push."

Lara screamed a bloodcurdling scream, and the baby's head popped out. "Is he OK? I don't hear him!" Lara was panicked.

"I got a head! We got a head!"

"I can't do this anymore. I can't do this. It's too hard."

"Yes, you can, Lara!" yelled Seth. "Listen to me.

Push as hard as you can! I got the baby! We came this far, one more push!"

This resonated with Lara. She propped herself up to get in a good position. Grabbing the passenger side headrest and backseat headrest, she pushed with all her might.

"Head, now shoulder, knees and toes…" Seth sang. He caught the baby sliding out.

"Oh, oh, oh!" exclaimed Seth with a shout of joy. "I don't believe this!"

"Oh my God," Lara said with pure and utter exhaustion. "Is he okay?" She heard mewling like a kitten and then an outraged cry.

"Hush, little one. Daddy loves you," Seth cooed, laughing and crying at the same time.

Seth quickly wrapped the baby up in the towel. "Is he all right?" Lara demanded, only to hear Seth reply, "She's beautiful. Perfect. I am so proud of you, Lara. I love you."

"Oh, Seth." Lara's eyes stung. "Are you okay?"

"I couldn't be happier," then to Marni he said, "Go into the glove box; I have a pocket knife and some duct tape in there. Give it to me. Let me cut the cord."

"Why do you have a pocket knife and duct tape?" "Jimmy."

Marni dug into the glove box. She removed a giant pocket knife and a roll of gray duct tape and handed it to Seth.

"Duct tape?" Marni questioned.

"I need something to clamp the cord."

He wrapped duct tape around the umbilical cord close to his daughter's belly making a tight tourniquet. Sighing, he then cut the cord.

"Seth." Lara was teary. "A girl. We don't have a name prepared."

"How about Cicada?" Seth responded with a smile.

"Oh, Seth. We have a daughter." Lara's eyes stung as she cuddled her daughter close.

"I am the happiest man on earth. You did good, real good."

"I like Hope." "What?" Seth asked.

"Hope. She's filled me with hope. We're going to be OK."

"Lara, she's gorgeous. Seth, maybe you should go back to school to become a doctor."

"I hate to break up the warm and fuzzies, but perhaps we should continue our joyride to the hospital? They have to clean Lara up," Seth stated.

"Let's go," Lara responded as Hope squealed. "The four of us."

"My brood," Seth said.

Lara enfolded her baby to her breast and stuck her nipple in the baby's mouth. The baby rooted quickly and aggressively. "Ouch!" Lara's eyes opened wide as Hope latched on to her.

Seth climbed over to the driver's seat. He put the car in drive. The lights flickered and then the whole SUV died. Marni turned on the camera flash. "What now?" asked Marni.

Seth checked the gauge. He was speechless. "I...I..."

"What Seth?" "I have no gas." "No."

"Seth, what do we do?"

Fate was setting in. It was enough with the setbacks, but at this point there was nothing more Seth could do. "I did everything I could. At least we'll all be together."

The girls began to sob. Lara looked deep into Hope's face, taking her in.

Seth removed the gun from the back of his pants. Everything stopped. Marni put the camera on the dashboard.

"Seth, what are you doing with that?" asked Lara.

"We won't feel anything."

"Seth," Lara pleaded. "We've come this far. Something will happen."

Seth's eyes slid shut, tears prickling behind the lids. "It can't end this way. It just can't." He didn't even realize he said the words aloud.

The worst-case scenario had happened.

He would shoot Marni first. Then Lara. Then Hope. Then himself. It was better than suffocating to death. It would be quicker. He didn't want his family suffering. There was nowhere to go, no one to call. Even if they tried to go outside, those things would swarm them.

He didn't know how long it would take to die from those things implanting their eggs inside him. It took Dominic barely a week. He had no idea how long it took Jimmy to die. He just wanted it to be quick.

Seth didn't want his family to suffer. That was one thing he always promised Lara, that he would do everything in his power to make sure they weren't in pain.

The glass started cracking from the weight of the cicadas. There was no more time left. He had to do it quick or they would all be crushed—or worse, crushed and still alive writhing in pain.

"I can't believe this is where it ends," Marni said in hysterics. "On the fucking Long Island Expressway."

Seth slowly cocked the trigger. He turned to Marni.

"I…I want to do it myself," Marni pleaded with tears pouring from her eyes.

"Are you really going to do it?" Seth asked. Marni nodded her head.

He handed the gun to her. "Just point and shoot."

"Like you've done this before," Marni wanted one last joke before her life was over.

"Marni!" Lara grabbed her shoulder from behind the seat.

"Promise me that you're going to follow."

She saw the glass cracking in the back. Another minute and the car would be filled to the brim with cicadas. They would be crawling into every orifice.

"I don't know where I'm going next, but I sure hope it's better than this," Marni said sadly. "See you soon."

She stuck the gun in her mouth. Both Seth and Lara squeezed their eyes shut.

Marni closed her eyes tight. Breathing hard, she touched the trigger gently.

Click.

Seth opened his eyes and stared in disbelief at the scene he saw outside through a small spot in the windshield of the car. "Noooo, Marni, don't!" He reached across the car to grab the gun.

Boom.

A liquid hit the car with furious vigor. The entire outside of the car was being pulsed with water.

Marni stared with wide eyes at Seth, who held the unused gun in his hand. She opened her mouth but no words came out.

"What's that?" Lara shouted over the roar of water hitting the car.

Light shone throughout the entire car. Beautiful, glorious sunlight poured in the windows. Marni was still.

"Can you see me?" she asked Seth, looking at him. Seth nodded his head, more confused than she was. "Are you dead too?" she continued.

Seth shrugged his shoulders. "Am I a ghost stuck in limbo?"

"I don't think you're dead, Marni." "How do you know?"

Seth grabbed the gun from Marni. He unloaded the clip and looked inside. It was empty.

"Your number wasn't up, Marni." He peeked through the clip in a playful way. "Only you could screw up killing yourself, Marni."

The deluge of water had coated the car. "Do you think heaven is a car wash?" They couldn't see anything else because water was streaming down the car. The cicadas were being washed away.

The gushing stopped.

There were two knocks at the window. All three of them yelped, their hearts beating frantically.

Everyone glanced over to see a blue-suited officer motioning for Seth to roll down the window.

At first Seth didn't know what button to touch.

He accidentally started rolling down the back window. "Sorry." He rolled down his window.

"Everybody OK?" asked the officer.

"Yes!" exclaimed Seth. "Yes! We were on our way to the hospital. My wife just delivered our baby. She's in the back."

The officer peered to the back. "You OK, ma'am?"

"Yes, yes, officer."

"Good. Stay put. I'll be right back."

"Wait, where are you going?" Lara yelled.

The officer left. Seth recognized that face. "Did he look familiar?"

"You know him." Marni looked on confused. "I think that was the same guy who…"

"Yes, it was," Lara said in tears. "What was his name? You made a joke of it."

"Simon. I said we had to do what Simon said," Seth said with a chuckle. "If I wasn't seeing him with my own eyes, I wouldn't believe it."

He knew everything was going to be all right. About twenty yards away was a water truck with a full tank washing the cicadas away. Five fire engines, a dozen army trucks, and four ambulances were positioned on the Expressway. The water truck and fire engines were washing the cicadas to make a path for the EMT workers.

The police officer returned.

"I wasn't talking on my cell phone, I swear," Seth told him, his hand on his heart.

This broke the ice completely. The back door opened. A team of emergency medical technicians swaddled Hope and helped Lara out of the car.

Marni grabbed the camera as she peeled herself off the seat.

An entire team of EMTs ran over with stretchers.

They hooked up Lara to an IV.

Seth exited the car, his knees suddenly wobbly, his gait unsteady. He looked at Officer Simon and the world wavered as his adrenaline rush subsided.

Drunkenly, he latched on the officer and gave him a bear hug. "I never thought I'd ever say these words. I love ya, man."

"You're OK, son."

Seth and the police officer came around to help Lara onto the stretcher.

"How's the baby?" Seth asked.

Officer Simon took the camcorder from the front seat and threw it into his squad car. Marni was led onto a stretcher, completely exhausted.

"How did you find us?" Seth asked the officer. "Once the army got involved, it got easier," he replied.

"My husband delivered our baby." "Nice work, kid."

"Seth was amazing." Marni sighed deeply.

"It was nothing, I swear," Seth said, blushing. "She did all the work."

"Well, we're going to get you all to the hospital. Is there anyone else with you?"

Marni looked down. "My boyfriend." She shook her head. "Where?"

"At our house," said Seth. "What's left of it." "We'll have some direction on how we're going

to kill these bugs over the next few days. But otherwise, let's get everyone loaded up and on our way."

"Thank you," Seth said and walked toward the ambulance to join Lara and his child.

Shirt plastered to his body, Seth pointed to the water raining down on them. "That stuff OK?"

"It's just water." Simultaneously, they lifted their heads up to drink. Seth stepped between the two stretchers and took both girls' hands.

Gallantly, he kissed them both on the wrists. "Nice work, my ladies. Couldn't have done it without you." He leaned down to kiss his daughter's sweet cheek. "You too, my little ladybug."

"Call her sunshine, muffin, sweetie but no bug names." Lara pulled his face for a lip-smacking kiss.

"She's as cute as a bug in a rug," he teased. "No bugs!" both girls shouted.

Marni was rolled to a separate ambulance, Seth and his family in another.

Jonathan Tate was standing with the EMT staff crew on the Long Island Expressway. Idling over to the squad car, he slipped in and took the camcorder. "This ought to be interesting," he sniffed. He began filming the departing ambulances. "Wonder what's on it," he said to himself as they drove away.

ABOUT THE AUTHOR

BORN AND RAISED on Long Island, Michael has always had a fascination with horror writing and found footage films. He wanted to incorporate both with his debut novel, Brood X. Earning a degree in English and an MBA, he has worked various jobs before settling into being a full-time author. He currently resides on Long Island with his wife and children.

michaelphillipcash@gmail.com